Idle Hands

An Anthology of Short Fiction

Other titles in the series:

Copyright 2007, Seneca@York

Printed by: Hume Imaging

ISBN: 978-0-9688182-8-2

Published by: Seneca College
Seneca@York Campus
70 The Pond Road
Toronto, Ontario
M3J 3M6

For Susan

FOREWORD

Seventeen books and counting...

I've said it before and I will say it again: the enduring value of this Creative Writing Seminar is its incredible ability to work magic with many of the students who come through the door on day one, those students who buy into the process and commit themselves to achieving something that, the moment before they arrived, they may not have thought possible. One need only read the stories collected in this volume, IDLE HANDS, or the stories collected in any of the sixteen volumes that precede it, to know this is true. In a world where the value of the written word, the value of knowing something about the structure of language and how to manipulate it, seems, at best, a negative asset or, at worst, irrelevant, these people have demonstrably flown in the face of conventional behaviour and affirmed their belief in that which is somewhat out of fashion. They worked hard to make sure that, in every way possible, their tales exhibited polish. So much so that many of them could be published almost anywhere.

In addition, the stories are insightful. I spent a great deal of time impressing on the writers the necessity of making their stories philosophically and experientially sound. They had to say something about the human condition and that which they said could not be without some depth. The idea was to make their readers think. Give their readers an intellectual challenge, not just an entertaining few moments. Certainly, in this respect, these seventeen writers have succeeded.

And they succeed in a variety of settings. From a traditionally lyrical and image-filled drama set in a mining town in Labrador to the fantastical landscape of the Middle Ages and the hulking tower of a depraved "undead" king, the stories draw you, the reader, into their worlds and shake you, now and then, to the roots of your being with ideas large and small. Stops are made in a pod where the end of life on earth is being discussed, in a driveway where a jilted lover is melting down, in the war-torn countryside of Eastern Europe, in the jungles of South America and in the "jungles" modern urban North America, in the political prisons of a third world republic, in the imagination of a railroad afficionado, in the tragic "flight" of a young drug addict, in the difficult if not impossible world where an attempt to revisit the past is made. Every story is a gem. Every gem shines brightly.

The writers are to be congratulated, heartily, for their accomplishment. Many of the tales you are about to read have been pored over laboriously. They have been rewritten and rewritten until periods were being removed and reinserted. It was then, and not until then, that their creators knew they were done...and done properly. So, sit back, take this book firmly in your hands, crack the spine (gently), and allow yourself to be enveloped by the worlds and ideas that will lay themselves open before you. Each deserves to be visited. Each deserves to be understood. You will be better off for the experience of going where these visions take you, just as I am better off for the experience of having been the teacher of these writers whose innermost selves are collected between these covers.

Professor Brian L. Flack
Seneca@York
January 2007

N.B. I would like to pass on a word of thanks to all the areas within Seneca@York that have been important in this book seeing the light of day: The School of English and Liberal Studies, The School of Computer Studies, The School of Communication Arts, The School of General Arts & Science, and The Faculty of Information Arts & Technology. In the absence of the financial and moral support offered by those who remain anonymous behind these titles, this Creative Writing Seminar would be no more than a good idea. In a more specific way, I would like to shine a light on the contribution of two people: Jackson Withrow and Josie Sage. Jackson, a student in the Creative Advertising program, in addition to penning a very fine contribution to this volume, also created the art for the cover. Josie, I would like, once again, to single out for special mention. A tireless member of the Seneca Printing/Media Production Department, she, thanks to her considerable computing skills, and the time her department allows her to devote to this project, created a beautifully designed text.

CONTENTS

IDLE HANDS
Lauren Jane Penney

Four years after she saw the explosion the world changed again. It brought her here.

* * *

She is not at the tree line anymore. No more bear threats or frozen nights. She is in this forest now. Where buildings are so alien in the sky that even birds smack into them, stunned and stupid. She belongs here, in this forest of glass and steel. Her heavy boots in gray city slush, her face refracted by windows and smeared by exhaust.

She is almost at home here, as she once was in the muffled silence of snow. Where the sky was an overturned bowl of dawn light, so big all the buildings of this city could not fill it. She wonders at times what happened to the horizon, now that these buildings join the earth and the sky. She believes the sun must be jealous of them, taking up so much space where it used to shine and shine.

* * *

The spring she turned six Labrador City opened eighteen kilometers of brand new highway. Thick, sticky, black tarmac reached out towards northern Quebec. She never saw that highway. She saw everything else though. Living in a place like she did, everything happened behind open windows. She never saw that highway because it was below the tree line and life below the tree line was a different world.

"There are guns under the beds here," her mother said, "and over the doors." Daughter and sister to life-long hunters, her mother knew a thing or two about guns. She could take them apart and put them back together with her eyes closed.

The summer that a highway provided a way out was the same summer as the explosion. Heavy and light blasts floating like weighted bathtub toys in solid rock. The mine's only purpose was to pump iron blood to civilization. So the earth's muscles were torn open and beaten back. Miners searched, like an autopsy performed by many, for great veins of ore. The smell was always of fresh earth, newly exposed and still raw.

When it rained the air was cold and sharp, like glass. The puddles were always shaped like the tread of the trucks and cranes, some four feet wide, and so deep her bare feet disappeared up to the ankle. Miners churned so far into old earth they disappeared, came back from the center of the world sparkling with dirt and sweat, tired and looking straight up, always at the sky, like a reflex.

To watch hundreds of tons of earth rush up and away from you was to know that it could rush towards you just as fast. A massive abyss in the earth came yawning into existence. The prelude was pillars of rock and dust, gushing up from the ground like blood, but black and burnt, filling the sky. The earth had a visceral reaction: it rippled like water. The pebbles under her bare feet, and everything miles deeper, shifted. Her heart locked tight in the hollow of her chest, stunned and stupid. The force of it moved through her and sucked all the air from her lungs, moved past her and slammed them full to bursting. The sound was so big she knew upon hearing it that, no matter how much she grew, she would never be able to hear it all.

Dust rained down for days. She thought they would all drown in it. Tiny glistening fragments of pebbles and ore landed in her hair and made her eyelashes sparkle in the sun. She could feel the grit on her tongue, cracking between her teeth when she bit down hard on her molars.

After the explosion she thought she would never be unaware

again; every step she took was barefoot and hesitant. She felt the soles of her feet connect with rock and earth and everything that grew out of it: cities that she had never seen, trees so tall they could only live in story books, all connected to her through the earth and the hard skin on the bottoms of her feet. For weeks she walked with fear, waiting for tremors, or shifting. For months she held her breath and watched the horizon.

Over time the fear became little more than something that haunted her during fevers. Her days were filled with cut knees and pet rabbits, and orange cream popsicles. It snowed from September to May, brittle air, and dead cold. Summers were brisk, thick with dark clouds, black flies, and scorched, dry wind. Years passed quickly and rainy Sundays lasted forever. Only sometimes did she wake in the early morning, quaking with fear and, then, when she opened her eyes, relief.

One such morning she woke from the nightmare of sound chasing her eyes open, but relief came slowly. It crept into her, wanting to keep its distance from fear, which was clinging to her skin like water after a bath. That same day her mother took her to the hills for a walk. Her mother was a beautiful woman who did all the voices in stories and entered every room like Spring.

Her mother worked sparse hours at the mine's employment office. She gave out colourblind tests. Administered mechanical aptitude surveys. She kept track of the paper work. Made sure no one who quit to collect vacation pay could come right back after his bender, broke from swimming in booze and sinking his snowmobile, looking a little yellow around the eyes.

There was nothing but space for miles around them, only roads to nowhere. With so much space it was easy to get lost, to walk off the end of something without even noticing. To wake up at the bottom of a bender and want your job back, just for something to do.

The hills were made up of horizontal lines, long and tense. Each layer of rock placed with mathematical precision, each one leading inevitably to the next. Here and there a line came jutting out in a manner that suggested purpose, suspended, giving the rock an appearance of weightlessness. Sometimes the lines became vertical, and it was sudden and jarring. A layer of rock just appeared, rising up instead of out, like a sinking ship.

The trees that grew on the hills were stunted and small. The hands of old men who have lived a life of work. Their branches carved squares and triangles out of the sky. There was almost no good soil at the tree line. What was there was stretched thin over rock and frozen earth. The ground was hard, unforgiving. Only a wispy, dry grass covered the ground in the summer, always more yellow than green, always too new to last long.

She knew, as soon as they had walked the first table of rock that something was different. The air was thick and hot, the wind came in gusts, strong but short-lived. The heat, though, seemed to come from the ground. She could feel it though the soles of her feet. The smell had the shape of something dark, something peripheral to her senses.

The sky was smudged. Living near an open pit mine, the sky was always smudged a little; dust hung in the air and stained the bottom of the clouds. The air at the hills, however, was usually wet with desperate life. But there, with her mother, she saw the sky grow dark, heavy, and move. The smudge was not under the clouds, but of them. Smoke had filled the air over their heads and her mother's calm, cool hand on hers was leading her up into the hills.

"We are safe; we do not have to run." Her mother sang it like a song. "But we should go up, then we can see." They climbed the hills like steps, going up past the trees.

Off and away from them was a writhing black worm in the sky.

The smoke rolled in on itself, swam up and out. Below the smoke she knew there should be trees, but there was only fire. Occasionally in the smoke there would be a lick of yellow, fire rolling in the air. It did not crawl forward; it leapt. From sparks sprayed by wind, or from the tongues of fire caught in the churning smoke, new spires of it would rise from the trees. This new fire would move forward, fueled by the fire behind it, rushing to catch up.

Her mother made her drink water and, after she rubbed ash from her eyes for the first time, took her hand again. She resisted, but only for a second. It was only after she turned her back to it and faced towards home, that she grew a little afraid of the fire.

The hills burned for weeks. They burned around the mine, filled the sky with smoke, and around the planes filled to the brim with water. Despite the protests of her father, her mother packed bags with water and condensed milk, crackers and tins of tuna. She put an orange and red reflective sticker on her window, so that if, "God forbid it happens, the fire crew will know it's a child's room and save her first."

Some people just packed their bags and left, driving off to places where there were no roads, or gas stations. The men from the mine quit their jobs. They walked off into the hills with shovels and work boots, with their wives kisses for a safe return. They dug trenches, mostly just for something to do.

When she came in from outside her skin was covered with a dust of black soot. Her ears were ringing from the muffled raging of the fire, a sound she was more aware of when she stopped hearing it. The sky collected the smoke, held it. Filling up and filling up. By the end of the second week the sky was so heavy it had sunk to just above their heads. Everyone stopped looking up and started looking out. They all stood outside their homes, looking off in the same direction. Their faces held fear, and soot. They watched. They waited.

The steps from the door to the street seemed too far a distance to walk through the heat. It swam under her skin. Standing outside, the ground was hot under her bare feet. Each pebble and grain of earth was charged with it. The heat became too much; televisions, radios, and stoves stopped being used. Boredom settled in with the smoke.

By the fifteenth night of the fire, she had become used to the sounds of it, the substantial roar and the snap of burning wood. Over the past few nights, they had been what she had listened for and followed into sleep. She woke because the sound had become erratic. The rush of the fire was still there, but softer, like it had been stuffed with cotton. When she managed to pinpoint the change in the sound, it took her a moment to recognize it. But as soon as she did, she could hear it all around her. She lay in the dark of her bed and listened: it was rain.

The sky had made itself a glutton with smoke, became fat and full. Rain, of course, had been the only possible resolution. They had all been waiting for it, but after fifteen days and nights they had all forgotten what they had been waiting for. The waiting had become an end in itself.

The fire ran itself out. It had spread too eagerly, too quickly, so it was snuffed out by the rain after only a few days of struggle. Her mother stopped sighing, started smiling again, and put Billie Holiday on the record player. Life, everyone assumed, was now supposed to return to normal. The pit had been waiting, neglected in the face of danger; it now appeared wider than ever. Once again the center of their world, it demanded that they all go back to work.

Her mother went back, sat at her desk and waited for the men to form haphazard lines so she could smile softly, sympathetically and say: "I'm sorry Mr. _____, but you only quit ten...eleven... thirteen days ago and you know the policy. Come back in two weeks and we can start you at your old salary."

* * *

The men grumbled, cursed under their breath, or bellowed out loud. They slammed their fat fists on her desk, leaned in close so her mother could smell smoke and beer and earth. She never stopped smiling; she smelled like soap and fresh water. She was a little wisp of milky skin and blond hair, so the men thumped out of the office, defeated by her size and pretty face.

Hunter Green had worked for the mine since it opened. His wife hated Labrador, hated the mine, and was so afraid of the fire she had packed up their Chevy truck and had driven off to nowhere. She had done this while Hunter was in the hills, digging a trench so he could tell his wife not to worry and actually mean it. She had taken everything, people said, their wedding album and all the pots and pans. People said she left her wedding ring balanced on the edge of the kitchen sink. The men called her a coward bitch. The women only smiled, wondered where they would put their rings if they ever left.

Her mother saw Hunter coming and had to force her face to form an expression of nameless sympathy instead of the deeply personal one she knew was worming its way to the surface. Hunter's wife had been gone for a week; he hadn't been at work for nine days. His beard was thick and black; the skin around his eyes and lips was yellow and paper-thin. He smelled only of liquor and desperation and rain. He was soaked from it and dripped water on the floor.

Her mother knew just by looking at him that this man needed to work. He needed his arms and back to hurt from it. The mine was the only thing he knew and he needed it now like little boys need their mothers. He needed to walk into the earth as though it were a grave and come back covered in ore dust like new skin.

Instead, her mother said, "I'm sorry, Mr. Green, but you have only been off the book for nine days, and you know the policy. Come back in twenty-one days and we will start you off at your old salary." She looked at him. The only move he made was to rest the tips of all ten fingers on her desk.

Her mother did not know Hunter Green. They went to the same barbecues. His wife had always brought brownies to union meetings, the ones from the box, but she added M&M candies. He always smiled, shook her hand with the same firmness she was positive he shook every hand with. He looked people right in the eye. Her mother, however, could not recall what kind of beer he drank or his birthday (May 23), though she knew she had been to at least four of the parties.

She did not know Hunter Green but she saw something change in him. The change did not happen in his eyes, or anywhere on his face. She was looking at his hands. His fingers were long, with knuckles like knots. Despite the sickness in his face, his hands looked strong and ready. They pressed into her desk so the nails were white, and she realized the only thing keeping him anchored there were his fingers on that desk.

As soon as she finished speaking, his hands slipped slightly. Blood rushed back to his fingertips, but he did not move them from the surface of the desk. The veins on the backs of his hands seemed ridged. Her mother looked away from his hands to his face. She tried to look him in the eyes, but they were set on the desk, between his hands, where drops of water fell from his hair.

"Hunter," she used his first name, hoping it didn't seem presumptuous, "everyone's tired. It's been a rough two weeks. Take a rest, most of the guys are."

Hunter didn't speak; he just nodded. His eyes met hers for a moment and he nodded again. Then he lifted his hands off the table. Her mother noticed that the gesture appeared almost as something he had to will himself to do. A conscious decision. He nodded a third time, dropped his eyes, and turned his body towards the door. As he walked out, her mother noticed that the cuffs of his pants were caked with black mud and she remembered, with a twist of sadness, that he must have walked there and was now going to walk back to his empty house. She had a vivid feeling of the cold in his bones.

More men came in, and left. Hunter's visit seemed to have left a residue. The men who came in no longer cursed or swore. Hardly any of them touched the desk and, if they did, it was brief, and they looked at it as though to clarify that it had been an accident.

Her mother was somehow not surprised when she looked up to find Hunter Green walking across the parking lot…not at first.

It took her a moment to become surprised, and then afraid. He carried a Kimber 1982, .22mm bolt rifle. Her mother knew enough about hunting to know it was a decent gun for buck hunting. She knew that if she could see the butt of the gun it would be checkered walnut, unless it was younger than an '82. Which it wasn't, she knew, as he lifted the gun parallel to the earth. The optical sight was a 44mm not a 48, another addition to the models following the '82 line.

Her mother watched as Hunter Green took his first shot in a standing position. She noticed how perfect his stance was, right down to the 45 degree angle of his hips, the easy rest of the stock in his shoulder. He shot over the pit. The first shot was followed by a second, then a third. Each one a crack of sound like rocks slamming down on a boy's hand.

She had slipped behind her desk; others in the bungalow office had dropped to the floor, and one of the men was cursing. Her mother didn't make a sound; she flinched slightly at every shot, her eyes squeezed tight. When one of the bullets came sailing though the window, she wondered if the glass had cut anyone.

She could tell by the sound of his boots on wet gravel that Hunter had moved, and was now standing somewhere by the shot-out window. He didn't say anything. Her mother could not hear him breathing, only sliding over the action release, a steady motion, like a breath.

* * *

Her father held out a bottle of Dad's root beer, as he always did, with an air of ceremony. As though presenting her something precious in the brown bottle with a pink bendy straw. He said something she could never quite remember. He lifted her up like she was nothing, mindful of her drink and her skirt. His arms were huge and his smell carried the memory of work, and outside, and something nameless, but sweet and dark.

Her father kissed her forehead, put his calloused fingers in her hair and did his best to smile. His eyes were watery and bloodshot, rimmed with red and swollen. He told her not to be afraid. He put her down.

They were standing in one of the five site offices. Little wooden shacks roofed over with corrugated iron, placed perilously close to the pit. The drops of rain made hollow sounds as they connected with the roof. She looked out the window and saw the water on the panes was black, soot washed off the buildings and out of the air.

Her father turned his back to her, his body resting on two hard fists pressed into a table top, his t-shirt slung loosely over two protruding shoulder blades. She waited for him to say something comforting, to dismiss her, or to cry. She waited, listening hard through the echoing drum of rain, but she heard nothing.

She stepped out of the shack and felt as though she would vomit. Root beer hot and churning in her stomach. The pit opened in the ground before her, a black gash in the earth. The wind was driving rain into her back and she was soaked through in seconds. She watched the rain and the trucks in the pit. She listened to the deafening force of the work being done all around her. She was appalled that everything continued…that the trucks remained upright and running, that people moved and spoke. She had expected a grinding halt. No one had ever told her in so many words that her mother was dead. But the fact that she was gone hung in the air, a fact bigger and darker than the pit in front of her.

* * *

Hunter Green had never thought of killing anyone. Especially the pretty young woman who had smelled so nice. But he knew, as soon as he shot the desk, that she was dead. She had fallen to the left and he could see her small white hand, fingers slightly curled. He could see the cuff of her blue sweater, and the delicate marble ball of her wrist. He knew he had killed her. Hunter did not eat a bullet because he felt bad for killing her…though he did feel bad. He shot himself because, looking at her little hand, he had wished it had been his wife's.

* * *

Her mother was cremated three days later. Her father did not speak, or work. He only sat in his suit, shiny at the knees and accepted handshakes and condolences. He nodded at the casseroles and pot-stickers. He drank until his hands shook and kept drinking until they stopped. She wore her mother's gloves, her scarves and sweaters; she slept on her mother's side of the bed next to her father, both of them exhausted and raw.

She and her father released the ashes in the hills, on the first day after the rain. Though the hills and been burned shiny and smooth, almost sculptural, there still appeared to be some force, both violent and serene, holding them together. The trees had been reduced to black balusters supporting the slate gray of the sky. They were smooth and still warm despite the rain. The trees were so black, made with straight lines and clean angles, that they looked as though they had been slashed into the scene with a knife.

Her mother's ashes blew away too quickly, got lost in a landscape filled with ash and soot and wet warm earth, still smoking in the distance. She held her fists tightly, and bit her lip until she tasted blood. Her feet were placed shoulder width apart; she used all her strength to keep them steady, to press them down hard. The rock below her feet was an upward thrust against the quaking of her limbs. She tried not to feel her body, just the clots of tension within it. Her stomach trembled, her arms and legs trembled, her lungs trembled. The rock ledges around her dissolved into long streaks of trembling.

* * *

They left Labrador that winter, and ended up here. The streets here are full of people. Each of them their own universe. An entire world locked away behind their skulls, tucked in briefcases, and folded up in the morning paper. Some stand in alleys, their eyes shining like dimes on the damp sidewalk. She wakes to the gray of dawn holding her, cold like stone, and smooth. She travels highways with four or five overpasses, stacked and staggered, curved and slanted.

A long street stretches out before her, it's buildings close together, so narrow they block out the sky like a canyon. She walks quickly, turning down a side street towards the lake. A lonely streetlamp hangs in the distance, a pregnant yellow dot in the steel sky.

THE HUMANITY EXPERIMENT
Conor O'Callaghan

The official records will indicate that America fell, of its own accord, somewhere between the years 2013 and 2020. Some people will tell you otherwise, but they are simply uninformed or they are part of the large group of patriots remaining scattered across the globe. Of course, America didn't simply disappear over night, but the fall from grace did happen quite suddenly and without much warning.

Some "experts" will tell you that they saw it coming long before it actually happened. They'll insist that all the factors were in place and that it was only a matter of time until the mighty United States crumbled beneath its own weight. Those same experts will tell you that America's foreign policy was seriously flawed and cost countless lives in what many dubbed "needless" wars. Others within the country would have justified the nation's actions as pre-emptive strikes against threats that could have taken it down, but the irony lies in the fact that the country was never able to eliminate the threats completely and in failing to do so, entirely, created new enemies.

Terrorism was a predominant theme of the new millennium, with several attacks being perpetrated on American and allied soil. Most notably, the 9/11/01 attacks against the former World Trade Center in New York and the Pentagon, the bombing of three football stadiums on November 11, 2011, and the symbolic nuclear strike against Pearl Harbour on December 7, 2018. While former Iraqi Dictator Saddam Hussein was captured in 2003 and sentenced to die for crimes against humanity in 2006, he was liberated by his followers before the sentence could be executed, an impostor standing in for him on the day of his execution. Then, from hidden locations, he launched several chemical and biological attacks on US troops. These caused countless more deaths before he was finally eliminated in January of 2008.

Osama Bin Laden was never found, dead or alive, despite endless efforts by the American military to bring him to justice. Al-jazeera, the Arab news network responsible for broadcasting his tapes in the post 9/11 fallout, reportedly had footage of Bin Laden's death and funeral, but it was never aired. While the United States maintained that Bin Laden was dead, new tapes continued to be broadcast shortly after every terrorist attack against Americans. While 9/11 stands as Bin Laden's most successful effort against the United States, he allegedly had a large part in the follow up bombing of the Empire State Building in 2010.

Following Bin Laden's lead, many other terrorist organizations attempted and succeeded in attacks against the United States. The undying Taliban continued to whittle down the American forces in Afghanistan and eventually the military withdrew all operations from the region. The Canadians, who sustained heavy losses, also withdrew, leaving Afghanistan in the hands of the Taliban. All the progress made within that country over the six years of North American presence was obliterated when the Taliban regained power.

The bond between Canada and the United States was shaken considerably by the failure in the Middle East, and relations between the long-time allies broke down. In addition, the United States border with Mexico was overrun with immigrants from the southern continent seeking to benefit from America's wealth. The sudden increase in population, combined with weakened resources at the military level, set the stock markets up for a fall, the nature of which had not been seen since the 1930's and the Great Depression.

It was about this time, July of 2012, that all of America's corporate corruption caught up to it. Insider trading, while making individuals rich, crushed some of the markets highest value stocks. In addition, the government's tendency to serve itself before the people suddenly backfired as the people rebelled against the failing democracy. Looting and rioting was rampant all across the United States. Canada closed its border and took a stand when desperate Americans tried to seek refuge.

After some of the dust settled in the wake of the economic crash, it appeared, however briefly, that America could return to normal. But when President Hillary Clinton—the first female President of the United States—was assassinated, America's fate was sealed. The backlash from that single event ignited a political free-for-all, and the country was divided into warring regions. With the United States plunged into chaos, dependent countries panicked and were assaulted by their enemies who, until then, had been too afraid of American retaliation. Israel could not withstand the assaults that it was defending itself against on all borders. Many other third world countries suffered the same fate.

The United Nations, while holding an emergency session, was destroyed by a rogue missile launched from an American destroyer, although it was later proven to be the work of a terrorist who had infiltrated the US military. All present within the building were killed. While the United Nations was considered a joke by some, its sudden destruction only served to increase the already widespread panic that had overtaken the globe.

It is not central to the history-altering fall of human civilization that has been dubbed the "Fall of Man", but the discovery of Area 51, The United States' famously secretive base somewhere in Nevada, caused another wave of panic. Strong-willed men who sought adventure and glory made their way there in hopes of discovering hidden technology or maybe something of alien origin. The weapons cache within Area 51 was ravaged by those looking to gain power, but only one man dared to venture into the deep underground labs to see what government cover-ups had been hidden there for decades.

It's unclear what happened first. The man, Steven Drake, as the records indicate, was a smart young man and so some people assumed that he unleashed the virus only after he had left the planet aboard a large alien craft that had been stored underground in Area 51 for nearly thirty years.

The virus unleashed was an unstoppable monstrosity that attacked the immune and central nervous systems of anyone that came into contact with it. It was determined, many years later, that it had been biologically engineered by the US government for an unknown purpose. While engineered by humans, its composition was not entirely of this earth. The virus' greatest strength was the micro-organism that, once the virus had been contracted, established itself within the bloodstream and eventually destroyed the victim from the inside out. It killed approximately 935,000 people across four continents within one year of its discovery. Nobody in the world had the resources to combat such a virus, and the only way to ensure survival was to kill anyone infected as quickly as possible to prevent it from spreading.

Many felt that this Infiltrator Virus was the product of a desperate government that had planned to unleash it against the world knowing that only it had the cure. A large portion of the population felt as though Infiltrator was the consequence and punishment for fifty years of decaying morality. AIDS had become prevalent due to widespread promiscuity, and bastard children—the ones not aborted—roamed the streets after being shunned to absolve their creators of guilt.

Sometime around the year 2030, the world's population was an estimated 750 million people. While the virus was still a considerable threat to anyone and was always on the verge of another outbreak, its spread had been contained mostly to Southeast Asia. In 2037, another brave man ventured into Area 51 to search the biological laboratories. What he found was a store of a solution labelled only as 1-X. After analysis, it was discovered that 1-X was the antidote to the Infiltrator Virus. Once again, America had an advantage over the rest of the world.

Out of the ashes that were America, a new world order arose under the strength of 1-X. The people united under John Cameron, a brilliant strategist who dreamed of rebuilding the United States to its former glory. He created New America, basing the new government on the principles of the old. The people rallied under this bold new leadership and Cameron's promises of safety and health inspired hope in everyone who heard his message.

By the year 2049, America had consolidated its dwindling power and hundreds of other countries and states were waiting patiently at America's doorstep for aid, but never received it. America had closed all its borders and nothing was allowed in or out. To the north, Canada was hit by the Infiltrator Virus but managed to persevere and attempted to rekindle the relationship between itself and the New America, but no calls were returned.

New American forces scoured the remaining portions of Area 51 and uncovered advanced technology that the old government had been suppressing. These discoveries led to a wave of technological advances in America, most notably with the automobile. The new discoveries also gave weight to the theory that America's wars in the Middle East and Iraq were indeed for financial benefit and control of oil reserves as many people had suggested at the time. Cameron insisted that New America would not follow the path of the former United States.

Stability in New America led to the redevelopment of programs for health care, education and space. Cameron was burning to learn what had become of Drake and his alien craft that had left Earth decades before. With the help of the new technology from Area 51, humans stood on Mars for the first time in 2074, after a month long mission. No life forms were found, but enough was learned of the planet to allow the groundwork for the first earth colony to be initiated. It would eventually be completed in 2117 after nearly forty years of environmental conditioning.

The human population had increased to approximately 22 billion on Earth and Mars by the year 2200. Cameron's successor Lester Smith began work to unite humanity on one front, but encountered heavy resistance from the European nations who were not convinced that New America was best suited to lead such a union, even with its advanced technology and superior knowledge of outer space and the solar system. New American satellites orbited the Earth as well as Mars on the lookout for anything foreign that might interrupt humanity's reconstruction.

Drake should have died no later than 2150, but his sudden and unexpected return to the solar system in 2231 heralded a frightening new possibility. Alien technology within the ship and genetic engineering now permitted humans an average lifespan of 200 years, nearly doubling life expectancy. People flocked to New America to be scanned and cleaned by the alien machines. The body purification process was the easy way to overcome the weakness inherent within a living body, immunizing and eradicating all known viruses, strengthening the immune system and cleansing the effects of things such as smoking tobacco or other substances.

Many had dreamed of immortality throughout human history, but this was the first step towards transcending death. Drake had given humanity its greatest gift and, at the same time, delivered its downfall.

With no disease and no shortage of food and resources, in short, with nothing to strive for, humanity was left with no defence against external invasions of any sort. Power and greed again became prevalent across the globe, as well as in the Mars colony. Humanity literally turned against itself, plunging the human race into a war that spanned two planets. Weapons of unimaginable horror were developed and unleashed throughout the solar system in an attempt to consolidate riches and territory, as well as to prevent anyone from escaping Earth as Drake had done over a century earlier.

Like a cancerous monster, humanity cannibalized itself and fell just as it had done 250 years before. With the harmful effects of radiation contaminating water supplies and food resources across the Earth, the population took another great blow, and massive cities were left empty, crumbling and decaying.

The civil war continued for over thirty years, until an alien craft particle-formed near Mars sometime around 2300. Despite numerous attempts to contact the unidentified visitor, none were successful, and no mercy was shown when a fiery beam emanated from the ship, vapourising the Mars colony almost entirely.

* * *

No records remain after that event.

We only found this record after extensive scans of the planet revealed several underground caches of a secret human organization that had documented the cataclysmic events. This report was compiled with extensive care from those studying it, and with the aid of a chronological program, rectifying all relevant data and updating the records accordingly. No remnants of the Earth race have been found.

It is still unknown why this colony failed so miserably. The greed the people exhibited was to a degree not seen before, and that is why they were terminated. No further experiments are to be conducted on Earth until the planet has been reconditioned and cleansed of the previous experiment.

Alexis Mayda
Serial 0129384729
Date 19/02/5402

THE DRIVEWAY
Sean Kelly

There's a car in her driveway, and it's not mine. I know it's not mine, because I'm in mine, across the street, looking at the car in her driveway. It's eleven at night and there's a car in her driveway. Why in hell would someone come by at eleven at night? The answer to that question is obvious, which is why I've been staring at this car for the past hour.

My eyes have drifted, occasionally, mind you, but not enough to escape noticing that only two of her rooms are lit, the living room and the bedroom. Of course, I could assume that the hall light is on, but I can't exactly see it from outside. I just know it would be, because you can't really see up the stairs without the light on, and she always has things scattered about. I know that well enough. Hell, I was there for most of the past four years.

I'll be the first to admit we were having trouble. That was obvious, but we could have overcome it. She just didn't want to try. I mean, people always change, that's just how life is, but the only way to get through it together is with compromise, communication, and all that other crap they tell you is supposed to work. I still assume that it would have but I wouldn't know because some people won't even give it a goddamned try. Kate was one of those people. It couldn't possibly have been her fault. If you asked her, she would say that she's the one who carried this relationship as far as it went. She told me that, but I didn't have the luxury of asking. I was simply told, whether I wanted to hear it or not. That's what she was like. She always had her way of doing things, and you had to abide by it, otherwise she'd get offended. Most of the time when that happened, she'd make this face. This ridiculous face that let you know she didn't agree with what was happening. You could see it in her eyes. She would change the shape of her mouth depending on the severity of the situation, but the eyes were always the same. Like the eyes of a thirteen-year-old girl who has just been told she's too young to get her ears pierced. She looks at you like you have no idea what you're talking about, and that only she knows what's right. Even in the simplest things. Like when we would go to the movies...if I chose a movie she didn't want to see, she'd get that face. Now I see that face in my head all the time and I feel like it will be the death of me.

I lied. I apologize. It's not a car. It's a truck. A simple slip-up, but I think once you understand that it's a truck and not a car you'll come to realize that it's a crucial piece of information. I came to some conclusions when I first saw that it was a truck in the driveway. The first is that the owner of this truck is likely a guy. I'm probably being stereotypical here, but girls don't drive trucks. That's just the way it is. So there's that on the table. Three weeks since we've been apart, and she's got a guy coming over to her house at this time of night.

The second conclusion I've come to about this truck is that this guy is nothing like me. I would never own a truck. The only guys you see in trucks are all brawn and no brains. The kind who were most likely jocks in high school and, if they weren't, were still likely to be pricks. I always figured she'd end up with a guy like that. They're easier to boss around. Nicer to look at. They're a woman's dream. Then there's me. I'd like to think that I'm not bad to look at, but then I like to think a lot of things that aren't true. I was always the kind of guy behind a computer rather than setting up at the line of scrimmage. I suppose I'm not making myself look too good, but I have my qualities. There was a reason why she loved me once.

I know she loved me. Sometimes you can be with someone

for a long time, and never know for sure if they love you. They can say it all they want, but everyone says it from time to time and doesn't mean it. There are only a few ways that you can be sure, and I knew for sure. Oddly enough I found this out during what I think was one of our biggest fights. On my way home from work, I got into a minor car accident. Nothing huge, but big enough that the police were called, insurance info was exchanged...you know the drill. It ended up taking two hours to get things sorted before I could get myself over to her place where I was supposed to meet her and, of course, she was right there waiting at the door.

As soon as I step in she blows up, yelling at me for not calling, her worrying, stuff my parents told me when I'd stroll in after midnight when I was sixteen. At first I was defensive. I told her she had no right to treat me like this after what I'd just been through. I was too busy to call. She should be thankful I was still alive. Basically just making it seem much worse than it really was, hoping I could win the argument. Somewhere along the way, though, I realized that she had been crying. Not because of the fight, but before I even got there. I also saw that the phone was still in her hand and I came to the conclusion that I was, as she had said, "an inconsiderate asshole," yet I couldn't help feeling really good about coming to that realization. I was only two hours late, yet she had been home with the phone in her hand, crying because she was concerned for my well-being. I don't think there's been anyone in my life other than my mother who's displayed that kind of caring towards me.

I genuinely loved her back, too. Everything about her. Not for the entirety of our relationship, but I know that for a moment, whether it was a year, a month, a week, or whatever, I truly loved her.

So, now it's one year since that day and I'm sitting in my car across the street from her house, while she's inside doing God-knows-what with God-knows-who.

For the first time since I've been here, a car is actually driving down the street. It's not surprising that it's not busy. This is a small residential area. I'll be honest, though. The car concerns me, so I quickly decide to busy myself with something in the glove compartment while the car passes, just in case it's a neighbour and they recognize me. I'd prefer to avoid an awkward stare as they pass if that's the case.

My left leg is falling asleep. I look at the clock; 11:33. Reminiscing really makes time go by fast it seems. As I step out of the car to get the blood flowing, I take a breath of the fresh autumn air. It's one of those nights, not too cold, just the type of weather you'd expect in late September. As I walk around trying to get some of the feeling back, I look up at the sky. I'm sick of staring at the bedroom window and that damn truck. As I arch my back and look at the cloudless sky, I feel a relieving ache when I hear my shoulders crack. I've been in my car far too long.

I don't know what I hoped for when I came here. It's almost like I wanted to catch Kate in this kind of situation. It's a lot easier to think about the past four years when I think of Kate as the enemy. Maybe I was hoping she would be waiting on her porch, just sitting there crying, wishing that I would come by, and then she would pledge her love to me again and everything would be great. Even better, I could come by and hear her confess to me the mistake she made, how wonderful I am, and then I could just spin it around, throw it back in her face and leave her regretting for the rest of her days what she'd lost. I hate to seem self-centered, but I think part of me actually thought that was a likely possibility. But showing up and finding another man's truck in the driveway certainly dashed any hopes of that fantasy becoming a reality.

For the first time tonight, there's movement in the window.

I see it out of the corner of my eye, but it is as though I have just witnessed a brutal car accident. I'm almost entirely frozen in place, standing outside my car with the door open. The only movement I can muster is the nervous quivering I feel from head to toe. I refuse even to blink unless absolutely necessary. I hadn't gotten a good glimpse the first time, but I wasn't going to let this slip away. I have to know what is going on, and the silhouettes behind the closed curtains are my only answer.

Sure enough, my stand-still patience pays off, and I see what I'm sure is Kate's silhouette pass by the bedroom window and, right behind her, like a dog chasing a bone, is the owner of the truck. Instantly, I realize that every single stereotype I had imagined about this guy from the truck has to be true. I can see that he's undoubtedly larger than I am, but I look reassuringly to my glove compartment to remind myself that, in a fight, I will have the upper hand.

With that thought fresh in mind, I begin to think about starting a fight. I imagine various scenarios, and each one provides me with the same gratifying ending: him lying on the ground with a bullet in his head, while I get off on self-defense or some other technicality. Or perhaps me and Kate running off to some foreign country since she'll fall in love with me again after I rid her of this parasite of a human being who's undeniably filling her life with anguish that only I can save her from.

I can't believe this guy would do this! It hasn't even been a month since we've been apart and he's already trying to move in on Kate, clearly trying to get her while she's on the rebound, most likely just to ditch her in the morning once she's given him what he wants.

He's moved in front of the window and hasn't moved for some time. Still frozen in the same place, I see him pull the curtain back. He looks at me, as I stand outside my car, illuminated by the dome light inside that hasn't turned off since I opened the driver side door. For a moment, we just stare at each other, neither sending any signals to the other. We have merely recognized each other's existence. I have no idea what he's thinking and he has no idea that I've once again been reminded of the 9mm in my glove compartment. I see his lips move briefly, and he puts the curtain back in place as he moves away from the window.

As soon as he disappears I get back inside the car. I know it's there but I have to check. I shut the door behind me and quickly search the glove compartment for the gun. I had originally planned to take my own life with this gun, in some melodramatic fashion to show Kate how terrible her life would be without me, but I soon realized the foolishness in that. Now I'm left with this gun. I had placed it in my glove compartment for no reason other than I had nowhere else to put it. Now I see it as fate. I put it there so that I could have this chance tonight to set the world right, to put things back in balance. An injustice has been done to me, and it has to be fixed.

For the first time since I got it, I hold the gun firmly in my hand with my trigger finger in place. I get a huge rush, like I hold the power of life in my hand. Only now do I really start to absorb the image of the man I have seen in the window. Goddamn pretty boy. He'll get his.

I quickly glance back up at the window for a few seconds. They're both passing by the window frequently now. Then all movement stops. A few seconds later, I see Kate move towards the window and start to pull back the curtain. I can't bear to look at her. Not yet anyway. I quickly fit the gun in the waistband of my pants, just above my back pocket, and step out of the car. Just as I close the door, the owner of the truck steps out of the house and starts walking towards me. I take a few steps and stand in the middle of the street, just watching him as he walks onto the curb.

"What the fuck man?" he says while looking at me incredulously.

I can't believe it! I can't believe that he thinks he has any right to question me being here! He should have come out and apologized, begged my forgiveness and told me how he could never live up to the standard that I have set for all guys who plan on dating Kate. If there were any justice in this world, that's what he would have said. There isn't any justice though, so I feel obliged to create my own. With that thought in my mind, I reach around, grab the gun, and point it directly at his face.

He's scared, and I love it. This is what I mean. This is justice as it should be. My hand is shaking violently, so much so that I'm concerned I'll shoot too early and not be able to enjoy this moment.

"Chill, man. Chill. It's cool. You don't need to do this."

Chill? Who talks like that anymore? We're well beyond our teenage years. This just pisses me off more, but as he says this I'm fairly certain that I see his eyes tear. It's all I can do to keep from smiling.

In my moment of glory, I look up to the bedroom window and see Kate. I don't know what I was thinking when I decided to look at her. I think it was more instinct than anything else. I wanted to see the woman I love. Never could I have believed that a simple look in someone's eyes would pain me as much as hers does. She is looking back at me, pleading silently. I have only ever seen this look once before. She stared at me this way during one of our fights. It's the look that I thought could only be reserved for me. It's the look she gets when she's concerned for the life of the man she loves. She's not concerned for me, though. Right now, there's only one man she seems to care about, and he's staring down the barrel of my gun.

In that instant, I realize I can't kill him. I can't do it to her. I look back at him and no longer feel any gratification for the fear in his eyes. I bring my arm down, and drop the gun at my feet.

As soon as I hear the sound of metal on concrete, I see the owner of the truck reach behind his back. I have been mistaken from the start. We aren't that different, he and I. We both love the same woman, and she brings out the worst in both of us.

He brings his arm forward and is now pointing a gun directly at me. I don't move. I don't even change the emotion on my face. I just stare back at him. I then slowly turn my head back up to the window and I see Kate looking back at me. Me and the owner of a goddamn truck. Who'd have thought we'd ever have anything in common?

As I hear the deafening crack, I realize that despite our similarities, there is at least one characteristic that he and I will never share. He is willing to pull the trigger.

SUMMER IN THE GARDEN
Anton Smolski

Intense summer sun was high over the lush land. Shade from a powerful oak did offer protection but hot, still air, pierced by sunrays that managed to find their way through the vast leaf cover lay like a blanket. When rare gusts of wind did rustle the leaves, it felt as if a sheet of warm silk had wrapped itself around my skin. Sweat, rolling down my face, stung my eyes and dripped off the tip of my nose. The midday heat was permeated by a strong crisp smell of wild flowers as well as aromas of blooming pear and apricot trees—so abundant in gardens and yards throughout this rich land. The quavering of birds and the incessant serenade of insects combined and made nature seem like a single living entity rejoicing in its glorious existence.

Through gaps between planks of the wooden fence, I peered at the beautiful land before me. The further I looked, the more the details of the landscape became obscured in the opaque haze of hot humid air. From the hill where I was sitting, in the tall, untended grass of an abandoned garden, I had a perfect view of the highway and the village below. On both sides of the road, rows of colourful cottages nestled in the thick greenery of gardens. Only their rooftops emerged from the leaf cover displaying a multitude of personalities in their dark red, rusted metal or bright orange and brown roof shingles. On the opposite side of the highway, the west end of the village stood on the shore of the beautiful and mighty Dniester. Across its glittering dark blue, and in places sand-shoaled yellow-green waters, lay Moldova, the land molded into multicoloured fields of cereals and neat rows of grape orchards, punctuated by birch trees and apple groves. These lands, east of the Carpathians, were a great garden—a gift of abundant natural wealth to the multitude of people who inhabited it.

I searched in the breast pocket of my jacket for a pack of Astra. I lit a cigarette and as I blew smoke into the planks of the wooden fence, my eyes fixed on the northern end of the road, about four hundred meters in the distance, where it disappeared around a hill. A thin cloud of smoke hung around me, slowly diffusing into the still air. I got through only a half of the cigarette before I threw it underfoot. From the north, two vehicles were quickly approaching the village. These belonged to the Special Unit of the Moldovan Police. As they came closer, I waved to the men crouching next to me beside the fence. I rose ever-so-slightly and flung up my assault rifle. I took aim. A few seconds passed before I squeezed the trigger, a short, controlled burst into the windshield on the driver's side of the lead car. As the weapon started fighting my grip, trying to climb into the air, a hail of rounds from both sides of the road began streaming down into the vehicles. In a few seconds, the lead jeep—its windows shattered, its hood and sides riddled with holes—skidded off the road and crashed violently into a telegraph pole. The other, after sustaining similar damage, gradually decreased speed and rolled another fifty meters past our position before it left the asphalt, pitched into the ditch, and rolled over on its side.

I crouched, changed magazines, and rose again.

"Nikrasov! Kostenko! Go from the left!" I yelled.

As I jumped over the fence, down onto the slope of the hill, two of my men, in paratroop camouflages and white sneakers, kalashy in hand, followed. On the other side of the road, two men emerged from the bushes and moved towards the vehicle smashed against the pole. Keeping my rifle to the side of my hip, I got down the hill and crossed the pavement to the ditch on the other side of the road. From there, I could see the bullet riddled slab of the windshield lying next to the car and a camouflaged body hanging half out the empty window, arms thrown about in the grass. I crept closer, the butt of the rifle now against my shoulder, my eyes and the barrel fixed on the back window of the car. No signs of life. I began noticing the hum of crickets again. Birds were no longer singing. I looked into the vehicle only to see the still body of the driver thrown by the force of the crash between the passenger seat and the roof. I came around the car to look at the body in the grass. His back was a dark red, his half-turned face disfigured by a grimace of fear, his eyes open and still. Kostenko stood guard on the road while Nikrasov climbed into the car through the front window to extract identification papers from the folds of the driver's uniform.

A single shot rang out from the back. I looked over to the other vehicle. Just a finishing shot. The two men standing by the destroyed jeep were now holding their rifles in one hand, barrels up, discussing the passports of the dead Rumyny[1].

The body of the passenger lying at my feet belonged to a sergeant in the Moldovan Army. What was he doing with a police unit, I wondered. Catching a ride?

"Well, you got into the wrong fucking car today," I whispered, my eyes on the pale photograph in the passport. I took the gun out of the holster on the dead man's hip and the ammunition he had on his belt.

"Did you check everything?" I asked Nikrasov.

"I got everything."

Through fine dust that had not yet settled from the crash, we walked towards the other vehicle and the men standing round it. They were chatting and laughing. They liked this war. Like Kostenko walking by my side, they were Cossack volunteers from the Don.

---

[1] A Russian term for a Romanian person - used by the local Slavs and their militias to refer to Moldovan army and police.

Our brave Dniester Guards, the first battalion, assembled just a few months back, were mostly volunteers from the local people of Prednestrovye[2], but also from all over Russia, the Ukraine and the Baltic. Even soldiers and officers from the Russian 14th Army stationed here were breaking ranks and joining the resistance. A whole engineering battalion under the command of Colonel Igor Dudkevich had joined our fight, creating the nucleus of the defense force in Parkany. The men who took up weapons and came to fight were real patriots, unlike the kings of the newborn fiefdoms that punctuated the Eurasian landmass with arbitrary borders. They cared not for our suffering. They, whose claim to their new seats of power rested on promises of leading the people to freedom and self-determination, had abandoned everyone here to the Rumyn onslaught. Kravchuk[3] had set up a fifty kilometer exclusion zone on the Ukrainian border with the DMR in order to stop the volunteers from arriving and picking up arms. But still the brave men came. Among these were the Don Cossacks who never forgot their pledge to Katherine the Great to defend Russia, its land and its people. Many in our Guard had fought before. I had fought duhi[4] for eight years—with my heli-born platoon, captured Panshir twice! Others had just recently returned from the Balkans to defend their own homeland.

Walking beside the desolate road I began to hear distant bursts of automatic fire and the muffled impacts of mortar shells. The front

---

[2] Russian name for Transnistria or Dniester Moldovan Republic (DMR)

[3] Leonid Kravchuk - President of Ukraine from 1991 to 1994

[4] A derivative term used by Russian troops in referring to Muslim partisans they faced in Afghanistan and later in Chechnya. The idea, propagated by a few western writers, that the term duh is Russian for "ghost" - referring to the elusive and frightening nature of the enemy they had faced in Afghanistan - is wrong. Duh is Russian for "spirit" or "soul" and, in this specific context, is derived from an Afghan-Farsi term dushman, meaning enemy, ironically adopted by the Russian troops. The Russian for "ghost" is prizrak.

line that sliced Bendery in half, just to the south, was rarely silent. I recalled a conversation with an old woman on the steps of a bakery in Bendery a few days before the Moldovan armored columns rolled in and began laying waste to the city. In her youth, she had lived through war and occupation. There was no fear or anxiety in her voice. She could not understand why Russia was not helping them in their hour of need. It seemed that everyone had abandoned her in the dusk of her years and her grandchild at the dawn of his. And not just them alone. Yeltsin had forgotten his people here and had forsaken the Serb nation—a loyal Slavic ally that had stood by us through numerous wars with the Ottomans and the Tauten—to carry the fight against the Ustasha[5] on their own. Mikola, who was laughing it up with Sharapov next to the crashed Rumyn car, had just recently returned from Krajina. He told many times over the gruesome story of how, after a pitched battle with the Ustasha and what turned out to be German mercenaries in Croat uniforms, they took back a Serb village around Medac. Terrible evidence of the cruel end visited upon the residents, who did not manage to escape before the village fell into Croat hands the week before, was simply the reality of that sadistic war. By the time Serb forces finally took Vukovar after weeks of stubborn Croat defense, the city existed only in name, its ruins like tombstones for the Serbs and Croats alike. There was no doubt in my mind that the Serb people would prevail in the face of the fascist onslaught like they had in the past, but through Yeltsin's inaction it would take more time and more lives.

While Christian Orthodox Slavs in the west agonized to stitch together what was left of their dominion, the gangrene of war set in, devouring my nation. Once united, it now lay like a dismembered corpse. Within the new borders, established with utter disregard

---

[5] Croatian SS division.

for the lives they would define, people burned, a dark victory for some.

"Mikola, how many dead?" I asked, looking at the crimson mosaic of the windshield glittering in the sunlight.

"Four. It's a fucking mess,"

"There was a survivor?"

"We did him a favour," Mikola replied, grinning.

The men around me were all smoking. I searched in my breast pocket. The pack was gone. Kostenko handed me a cigarette. I nodded and turned to a tall man in camouflage pants and a black Adidas shirt. He was flipping through passports next to me.

"Sharapov, go tell Valohin to get on the radio and call the armour. We're out of here."

As I took the bloodied passports from his hands, he saluted and ran across the road and up the hill.

"Tell them to keep sharp up there and to watch that fucking road!

Breathing smoke through my nostrils, I looked through the photos of the dead men in the car. I asked Mikola, who was again joking and laughing with Kostenko, which of these belonged to the driver. He pointed at a photo of a young man. He couldn't have been more than twenty years of age. Nicolae Cuza had brown hair and dark brown eyes.

"Don't stand around. Get back to the positions and stop all that goddamned chatter."

Silently, the men complied. They were good fighters. They just liked what they did too much.

Holding the young man's passport open in my left hand, gripping the rifle by its magazine with my right, I walked around to the driver's side of the ruined car and peered inside. Bodies. The driver was flung over the steering wheel; what was left of his head was resting on the dashboard. His face was unrecognizable. As I looked at the pools of blood, flies already buzzing around the dead man's head, I kept thinking to myself that I would waste another hundred brown-eyed Nicolaes just like him to prevent these loathsome forces from reaching out and threatening my old mother's happiness, my young sister's innocence. The only family I had – my mother and Vera – lived just fifteen kilometers from the war, in Tiraspol[6].

I recalled one night that I lay awake listening to muffled whispering through the darkness. In my underwear, I came out into the hallway. I recognized Vera's voice coming from the guestroom. She was on the phone. I leaned against the wall and caught bits of her conversation that reached me in the darkness outside the room. She tried to hold back her tears as she spoke to, what I understood to be, her lover. I never knew she had been seeing someone. Vera was scared. Scared of losing him. She didn't want him to fight. Every man in Vera's life she loved was leaving to go to war. She understood, however, that the terrible had to be done. And the man on the other end knew he had to perform his duties to his nation, for her.

When she hung up, Vera stayed in the room sobbing quietly. So we sat—she on the couch, overcome with grief, not aware of my presence and I, squatting in the darkness unable to leave my sister to her pain.

The next morning, I kissed Vera and my mother goodbye and reported to the command Headquarters in Dubosary. Since that day, I had never let the rifle out of my hands and the only way I traveled was atop the armour of our troop carriers.

I couldn't look away from the destroyed body, flaccid against the wheel. This man had tried to take away my language, my culture.

---

[6] The capital of Prednestrovye.

In May, it became absolutely clear that Snigur[7] would not abandon his fascist intentions towards Prednestrovye. In the course of the proposed Moldovan unification with its co-ethnic Romania, all Slavs were to become subservient and to these ends Chisinau was not going to refrain from using force. We saw what had to be done and we acted with ruthlessness. We pre-empted the threat. Two bridges across Dniester were blown up. Later, I led one of the simultaneous raids on three Moldovan police stations on our side of the river. If need be—if the 14th Army would not step in to protect us— the whole industrial capacity of the DMR would be turned to war production. We were ready.

Sharp whistling brought me back into the midday summer heat. I turned around and looked at the bushes on the hilltop. A faint rumbling of diesel engines was coming from behind the cottages.

"Our ride!"

I waved to Kostenko with the hand holding the passports. I tried to stuff them into the pocket on the inside of the jacket but in my haste the papers slipped from my grip and fell to the ground. I hung the rifle behind my shoulder to free my other hand and crouched down to collect the documents from the grass. Sticking out from between the pages of the driver's bloodied passport was what looked like the backside of a greeting card. It said, "To my love, Nicolae". I flipped it and, from the photograph on the other side, Vera's beautiful blue eyes stared into mine.

---

[7] Mircea Snigur – president of Moldova from 1990 to 1996

RAGE
Leona Lutterodt

Mark was in the kind of sleep that only jet lag could induce. His head lolled dangerously (or so it seemed) to one side. Janna kept worrying he would knock his head on the side of the doorframe if she went over a bump or took a fast corner.

Serve him right.

She had been looking forward to a quiet weekend when he'd called, out of the blue, saying he had arrived at the airport and needed a place to stay for a while. Just like that, no warning or anything. And of course, he needed picking up. She wondered what it was about her that made him feel he could flit in and out of her life on a whim. The worst part was that she had actually missed him when he was gone.

No, that wasn't entirely true. The worst part—her greatest source of irritation right now—was how overjoyed she was that he was here at all.

She looked over at her passenger while chewing at the nail on her left thumb, trying to soothe conflicting emotions.

Above the obsidian orb that was Mark's left eye, a tiny red light blinked each second. So much for taking the scenic route, then.

Janna wished he were awake.

At the next stoplight, she leaned over and waved a hand in front of him. She wanted to see if the gentle movement of air would wake him, but there was no reaction. She sat back again, deciding to appraise this new look he'd come back with.

His wavy chestnut-coloured tresses had been formed into six or seven dreadknots at the top of his head, and everything else— everything she used to run her fingers through—had been shaved

> 37 <

clean off. She didn't know how she felt about that. After all, he'd thrown a fit when she'd cut her own hair and dyed the tips of the short spikes red. A red that, he complained, registered awfully on his eye, like a bright magenta or something.

She wanted to trace out the new rectangle of bristles framing his mouth and chin. It was definitely...hmm...desirable, even if it did make him look older than his thirty-four years. Janna stared at the new goatee and wondered how long it would take to get used to.

Itchy abrasions.

She noticed, at length, the slight tan, and wondered how on earth she could have missed it. The Singapore sun, no doubt.

Suddenly, a cacophony erupted around her. Cars with Snarling Hoods crumpled back in grotesque mockery, jeered at her. They bared their capacious engines at her Nissan Glowe. Insult sirens set to maddening frequencies and sound patches with a choice mix of profanities made her understand.

"*See* the lights, damn it!" The Honda behind her spat the lyrics twice; the low-slung bass-line and crisp hi-hat of last year's nu-Raggamuffin hit rode above the other insults courtesy of a subwoofer from hell. Janna wondered what could possess someone to ruin a perfectly likeable tune.

"See the lights, damn it!"

She was flustered, and the shift stick in her Nissan finally overrode her fumbling, throwing itself into first...

"C-C-C-C...see the lights, damn it!"

...then a swift second...

"D-d-d-damn it! Whatcha waitin'..."

...finally third, and the Nissan's little tires screeched through the intersection.

The Honda swerved, black snake, to level beside her in the

left lane. Its windows de-paqued at a fantastic speed; the expensive dark-to-light transition hinted at one thing: A Rider.

It was all Janna needed after a long drive from the airport in halting traffic.

The Honda kept pace alongside, and the man inside was gesturing furiously. She wouldn't look, of course. She would… NOT…look!

But she could sense the other driver, that female peripheral vision thing.

Honda Man saw that the crucialness of his message wasn't getting across. The de-paqued windows slid down completely then to reveal him in the flesh.

"Hey, man! Ipfhu don know how to drive, jasstu stay outta fucking way, man!"

The Nissan's external microphone pickups spelled out Honda Man's message in crystal clear tones, cleaning the signal dutifully for her listening pleasure. The real sound still reached her from outside, muffled by the noise of traffic.

More gas, Janna thought. Anything to put some distance between her and this raving lunatic.

"Hey! You don fuckin' diss me, man!" said the Honda's speakers, just as the black shape glanced off the left fore side of her little Glowe, making its headlight blink shut protectively.

That was it. That was it!

Janna retracted her own glass barriers, at a little under the speed with which the red heat swept up through her bosom and exploded in her head.

"You can go FUCK yourself, okay?" Her arm, tendons sprung like steel cables, middle finger extended in rigid defiance to coincide with the 'uck'.

A torrent of some oriental dialect washed back at her, fluid and flippant in contrast with the warm, polluted breeze.

"...because of the stupid red light? Get OVER it!" Janna revved again to get away, losing handling for a split-second before rallying up the road.

Honda Man wasn't having this. He quickly re-synched the two velocities, lining up the open windows, struggling to shorten the vital umbilicus of rage by leaning across his non-existent passenger.

"You wan I tay-ku you opf road? Huh? Huh! You wan?"

She was incredulous. "How much more of this crap are you going to..."

"I tell you jasstu stay out my fuck way, man...stupid bitch!"

"I AM out of your way! You've got a whole frigging lane to yourself!"

"Hey, hey...HEY!"

Mark, not so asleep anymore.

He had been yelling voice commands to get the windows back up and re-instate automatic drive; Janna almost hadn't noticed.

The little car complied, taking over the controls and inspecting its destination co-ordinates. It turned at the next corner and sped up a little.

Mark reached toward Janna, making sure he had a grip on both her arms, and turned her towards him.

"What is wrong with you?"

"Nothing!"

Even as she said so, Janna felt her anger densify, reduced as it was to the space between their faces. Mark did not let go.

"I hope you don't do this shit when I'm not around," he said sternly. "You could get yourself killed."

Mark's other, natural eye was like looking into a blue fountain on a clear day. But it was completely useless—had been since he was born. Or so he said. Who knew, with Mark?

"I'm sorry, but…that guy was a complete frickin eejit. Christ, it was just a red light!"

"Easy. Just…easy, okay?"

Mark stared blankly at her awhile and then let go, slumping back down into his lack-of-space curl in the passenger seat.

Janna turned her attention back to the road. She didn't know where the Honda had gone, but the scenery flowed past in rich autumn colours, until they entered her own neighbourhood. She was about to breathe out in relief, when she saw something new in the rear-view mirror.

"Oh *God*."

Something like a disorderly motorcade closed in on them from side streets they had passed seconds ago. A subconscious calculation of speed and distance told her to start panicking.

"Mark!"

He straightened once again in his seat.

"There's lots of them now!"

"Lots of what?"

"Riders, Mark. Riders! Switch your bloody Gaze thing on, will you?"

Mark pressed a finger to his left temple and the blinking red light turned to a solid green. He turned in the cramped space to look out the rear windshield. He saw what alarmed her and cursed softly under his breath before ordering her to pull over.

"What? What are you doing! We can't stop now?"

"Auto. Pull over!" he commanded again, and the Nissan Glowe signalled right, pulled alongside the curb, and came to a halt.

"Mark, this is insane…" Janna was shaking her head. "…we should be calling the cops or something."

Within seconds, four or five cars had screeched and swerved into formation around them, revving needlessly, hoods peeled back, grills formed into customized chrome grins. They revved up a storm of blue smoke as tires spun on the asphalt.

Other cars clung to the far side of the road, spontaneously evolving a local traffic system to allow everyone else to get by and stay out of trouble.

Inside the Nissan Glowe, Janna had cancelled the Glowe's audio feeds because the noise had been unbearable. She had tried locking the doors only to find them unlock themselves each time. Someone out there had captured and descrambled the security keys to her car. She wanted to scream.

"Mark, *DO* something!"

He had been strangely quiet.

"Mark? Maaaarrrrk!" Janna hadn't meant for him to step outside, but he had.

She turned awkwardly in her seat, afraid to remove the seat belt, aware of how pointless the contraption was in light of the unlocked doors. But it wasn't herself she was concerned about right now. She looked through the back window, and something drained from her when she saw that Honda Man was there again. He'd stepped away from his car, and now strode toward Mark in his black jeans and grey shirt.

Should she go outside and try to help?

Oh God, Mark. I'm so sorry.

She didn't understand the communication that was taking place, but she was glad of it…glad for the absence of much worse.

Mark's back was to her; all she could make out were the glances that fed around the loose circle from Rider to Rider. Two of them leered at her.

Bastards.

Those two looked all of sixteen years old, if that.

She looked again and saw Honda Man was laughing, hard.

He was turning to go, making a strange signal at Mark, like taming a bull, forefinger and last finger pointing out of a fist. The Rider raised an open hand in the air and the others spun their cars one last time for show. Janna's relief was palpable. They were going!

They were going and, of course, the cops were coming.

What was it they said about crime in the city these days? It was like bad sex.

She could hardly believe the statement Mark offered up when questioned about the cars that had just left. But the uniformed men dutifully wrote it down and bade them farewell—a bit too cheerfully, Janna thought.

What was going on with the world?

It was a very quiet drive to her apartment. Mark wasn't sleeping anymore, but he wasn't in a chatty mood, either.

* * *

Mark stepped out into the night at 2:00 a.m. The yellow lamplight made his view a sepia-tinged old photograph, updated a few times a second. The flicker was noticeable, and that was why he sometimes just preferred to switch the thing off.

Tonight had been a strange night. When they'd gotten to Janna's home, she'd completely fallen apart on him. He'd half expected it though. Had to come after all these years of non-committal fucked-up-ness on his part.

His part...in all this.

How strange that in one night, love thought lost and love made were not enough to prevent him from walking again into his past, sliding into the driver's seat of a Fanged Jaguar left there for him, and speeding toward a promise he had made.

As the engine's hum rose to meet his demands, his vision shook; road markings, pavements, odd pedestrians, traffic signals—

everything fed into a pattern recognition circuit that he'd had to hone since childhood. Separating things that could be run over, and things that could not. It needn't have felt this familiar, but it did.

He began to laugh, loudly, and with complete abandon.

"Whooooo-hooo!"

This one is for you Janna, he said to himself.

But it was a lie.

Someone owed him the only good eye he ever had. And the man in the Honda might as well be the one to pay up.

THE BANANA IS ALWAYS WHITER ON THE INSIDE
Lam (Tom) Truong

The noise was deafening as I dropped the big cardboard box of motherboards. It was very heavy and I had trouble carrying it. When I tried to pick it up again my boss, Howard, saw me and I dropped the box again. He scolded me. "Hey be careful with that box...it very soft, easy to break!"

My voice trembled as I spoke, "I'm so sorry. My hand slipped."

"After clean up, get started on computer on technician table." He spoke with a thick Chinese accent.

I had worked in his small computer shop for two years. How I came to this job was indeed lucky. It was all because of a coincidence. Howard and I belonged to the same clan association. When we met, we became friends instantly, and he offered me a job as a computer technician. The store was in the heart of Chinatown, a four hundred square foot room. From the first day I worked for him, I considered Howard a friend rather than a boss. But now, in my second year there, the warm feelings of friendship were beginning to fade. I had begun to realize that I was just an employee in his business.

The technician's table was messy. Screws and computer parts were all over it and it didn't matter how much I worked to keep the table in tip-top shape, it always became messy the next day.

My co-worker Aaron also worked on the technician's table. He was a skinny and quiet person. Often I didn't know what was on his mind because of his quiet nature. He was also Howard's business partner. They both came from the same place, Shantou in the Guangdong province. Neither spoke English very well. Mandarin was their native tongue.

After I cleared the clutter from the technician's table, I started working on a computer. I knew what the problem was immediately. The memory modules were loose and didn't have a good connection with the motherboard. I knew the memory module needed to be inserted properly. It made a loud snapping noise as it latched into place. I turned on the computer and, as if by magic, the machine showed signs of life.

When I had finished the job, Howard came to me with my new task. He pointed at another machine. "You go outside and blow dust off computer."

I nodded and grabbed a can of compressed air. While I held the can, I dragged the heavy computer to the front of the store. Aaron was rushing and, as usual, he was late for work. He chuckled, "Hey, John, some cleaning? How bad?"

Looking inside the computer, I grimaced at the thought of the dust flying all over. "It's pretty bad; it actually has dust bunnies inside!"

Aaron laughed. "Good luck, man."

As I aimed the can of compressed air at the open cavity of the computer, I prepared myself for a gust of dust blowing my way. When I was about to press the trigger, an elderly Chinese man started to scold me. All I knew was that he was speaking in Mandarin, a language I couldn't understand because, as a Canadian-born Chinese, I didn't know it at all.

The elderly man soon gave up scolding me. He knew from the blank expression on my face that I didn't know what he was talking about. Ignoring what he said, I began dusting out the computer. The dust looked like smoke floating up in the sky. Trying my best not to breathe in, I covered my mouth and pinched my nose.

When I got back inside the store, I saw that Howard and the

elderly man were in conversation.

Howard addressed me: "Hey, when you blow dust from computer…don't dust near store's door. Customers don't like dust in face."

"Sorry about the dust," I said to the elderly man, but he didn't accept my apology. He didn't understand what I was saying.

Just then a frail man came into the shop and greeted me with a smile. "Hi John. How you good today?"

It was Henry, the programmer of the computer shop. He was a middle-aged man who, only three months before, had emigrated to Canada. His skills as a C programmer were great but his hardware skills weren't terrific. I didn't know much about Henry since he didn't speak fluent English either. We usually stayed away from each other because we couldn't really talk. At times, I tried, but mostly we just ended up frustrated.

I tried my best to decipher his message. I assumed that he was greeting me. With this in mind, I replied so that he would be able to understand. I smiled. "Hello, I'm very good today!"

After Henry received my answer, he nodded and began working on his computer in the office.

By 2:30 p.m. the small shop was empty and I found myself doing nothing. There were no computers to fix. Howard saw me and said, "Not much to do, go take lunch break."

I was hungry so I accepted his suggestion. "Sure, I'll go for my lunch break," I said.

I decided to go to the Golden Stone Restaurant. I was looking forward to a plate of stir-fry beef with vegetables and rice.

The restaurant was packed with people enjoying their food. The scent of fresh Chinese cuisine was in the air. The wondrous smell made me hungrier as I anticipated my favorite dish.

I signaled the waitress that I wanted one seat. She pointed to a table big enough for at least ten people. I would have to share the space with other patrons. I shrugged and went to one of the seats. The waitress came over to me and began talking in Mandarin.

I said nervously, "I'm sorry, I don't know how to speak Mandarin."

I felt embarrassed not knowing how to order in Chinese. After all, most of the authentic cuisine on the menu couldn't be ordered in English, and my favorite dish was no exception. As I tried to find the dish on the menu, the waitress waited impatiently. "So, what you want?"

Putting down the menu, I said, "I'd like to have the beef with vegetables and rice."

After hearing my order, she went into the kitchen and placed my order. A few moments later, she brought me a teapot full of hot Jasmine tea and a teacup.

After I had sipped all the tea, the waitress came back with my meal. As she put down the plate full of food, I looked at it without interest. I expected beef with bok choy, doku mushrooms, and ginger, but instead I saw beef, carrots, celery and snow peas in a red sauce.

While looking at the dish, I asked the waitress, "Is this my dish?"

The waitress replied, " Yes, this beef with vegetable and rice."

Knowing that they had misunderstood my order, I decided not to protest. I was too hungry and any kind of food would have been suitable at the moment. The dish satisfied me, but it wasn't what I had expected or wanted. It wasn't authentic. The sauce tasted like something better poured on McDonald's McNuggets, sweet and sour; the carrots were undercooked and hard; and the celery had a raw taste. Although I enjoyed the food for its filling value, I didn't enjoy its flavour.

Shortly after I finished, the waitress came over and gave me the bill. I opened my wallet and took out seven dollars and paid. I figured that I'd let them keep the change since it was late now and I had to get back to work.

When I got back, Aaron and Howard were talking. I didn't know what they were saying but I knew they were talking about me. They mentioned my name several times. This made me nervous.

After their conversation was finished, Howard began talking to me in English. "John, you understand?"

Oblivious to what they had said about me, I said, "No, I didn't understand."

They both laughed and Howard patted me on the back.

I didn't like being the one who never understood what was going on. Since the business was located in Chinatown, most of the customers spoke only Mandarin. I often felt that I was part of a puzzle that didn't exactly fit in. Although I was Chinese, I wasn't "Chinese" in the eyes of my co-workers or the customers.

I felt very uneasy. They had been talking about me...right in front of my face and I couldn't understand what they were saying. I wanted to know badly so I could also be in the conversation. But I lacked the language skills. All I could do was stand there and be oblivious to the joke.

Not being able to keep my cool any longer, I asked Howard, "What were you guys talking about?"

Howard looked nervous and said, "Nothing." Then he walked back into the office to continue his conversation with Aaron.

* * *

Just before seven o'clock, closing time, I started my clean up of the technician's table. By the time I finished, it was time for me to leave. I signed out on the time sheet.

As I made my way to the front door, Howard stopped me in

my tracks. "Hey John! Tomorrow you don't come. Take break from working. I call you back when I need you. Just wait for call."

Shocked that I was being laid off, I needed to know the reason. So I asked, "How come?"

Howard explained, "No computers to fix, so take break. I call in one week."

Knowing that he had made up his mind, I went home to wait for his call.

* * *

Two and a half months passed and I didn't receive a call from Howard. Fed up with waiting, I decided to pay a visit to the shop to see how things were going. Since I hadn't been in the store for two months, things had changed. Henry was now working as the computer technician and a new person was working with him, teaching him how to install a motherboard.

Howard saw me and greeted me. "Hey John! What you doing here?"

"Nothing, I just thought I'd visit my *favourite* computer store."

Howard signaled me into the office.

"John, I speak with you in the office."

Knowing that this was going to be serious, I said, "Sure."

I went into Howard's office and waited for him. The waiting made me anxious because I didn't know what he wanted to talk to me about.

When he came into the office, he closed the door behind him. "John, I know you wait a long time. I'm sorry I no call you. I forget. I replace you with another person, a Mandarin speaker."

I wasn't that surprised because part of me knew that eventually I was going to be replaced by someone who knew the language. I was just angry with Howard that he didn't tell me sooner so I could get on with my life.

I tried to maintain my pride like any other Chinese person would. I kept as calm as possible and lied.

"Howard, how could my position be terminated if I am here to quit? I found another job already and I don't need your job anymore."

I could tell that Howard was relieved.

"Oh, good you find a new job! What now?"

I was unemployed; I didn't have a job, so I kept lying.

"Oh, I'm working at the Nerd Squad Computer Store as the lead technician."

Howard replied, "Oh, that is good, that is good."

An uncomfortable silence ensued.

Finally I said, "Well, I'm going to go and pack up my things now and leave."

"Alright John, maybe one day we see you in the computer store as customer? Ha ha..."

I didn't see what was so funny that he would laugh. I had been replaced. Hell could freeze over before I ever stepped inside the store again.

Knowing that my role in the computer store was now a thing of the past, I opened the office door and went to collect my tools. Then I left the store.

Henry and my new replacement both said goodbye, but I didn't reply.

* * *

Two more months have passed. I have found another job. Unfortunately I wasn't able to find a similar position as everyone wanted a reference from Howard. And since Howard wasn't picking up his calls, I had no chance at an IT related job.

Even though I had every right to complain and fight for my

position at the computer shop, I decided not to. Seeing how Henry and the new guy relied on Mandarin, I took pity on them. I knew that, if they were to lose their jobs, they wouldn't have any chance of finding another as their English was well below the accepted standard. In fact, the way I saw it, they were like pets trapped in an artificial environment. If they were to pursue a job outside Chinatown, it would be harder for them due to their language limitations.

These days I'm working part-time at a burger joint. Even though the pay isn't as high as the job I had in the computer store, I still prefer it because all the staff speak English.

For now, I will enjoy my time at the burger joint, cleaning toilets, frying burgers, and making change. After all I am Canadian first and Chinese second.

THE UTOPIST
Jackson Withrow

Owen's car billowed smoke while it sat, idled, in the lonely unkempt parking lot. He released his foot from the gas just enough to hear the weathered gravel and stones churn under his tires. After appeasing his affinity for sounds only heard when there was absolute quiet, Owen put the vehicle in park, turned it off, and stepped out.

Before him was "Big V's Burgers". Owen remembered it all too well. An independently owned, wholesome-natured diner that was something of the epicentre of this old Kawartha town. The sign atop the structure could no longer identify the place to strangers in the area for neglect had eroded its appearance and function...much like the parking lot. For a moment, Owen's attention was turned to the picnic tables. He grinned as he opened his mind and brought forward the memories he had come there to reflect upon.

"Dani Traxler..." Owen allowed her name to escape his mouth.

There was no one around, nobody to watch him or to hear him actively remember a name. Maybe Owen was a bit surprised that the picnic tables remained, but that didn't prevent him from sitting at one to help recall and feel what he had come for.

"Can I buy you lunch? Eat lunch with you?" Owen remembered asking, with a small amount of reluctance. Or was it shyness?

"Well. Sure," Dani had said, adjusting her glasses. *"I did order already though. Burger and fries."*

"Okay. So they'll call you and I'll...yeah, okay, I'm going to get something too so I'm just gonna go order really quick," Owen

replied as he stood up. *"I'm Owen."*

That day, the sky was bluer than Owen had ever imagined it could be. Normally, to him, memory distorted colour schemes, exaggerated motion, and made environments increasingly abstract. Not that one, however, not any of the times he had spent with Dani. He could vividly recollect swimming in the lake with her, picnicking in the park with her, even her just walking towards him or away from him.

Owen's leather coat crunched slightly when he raised his hands to his shaggy hair. He stared fervently at and around the boards that had long been keeping people, mostly vandals, from making a mess of this ramshackle, derelict building. Aside from making an effort to detour and drive through this area, past this place when the opportunity arose, this was the first time in several years Owen had stopped. In truth, this was the first time Owen had brought himself face to face with "Big V's Burgers" since it was no longer an operating establishment. Today, he was there because a fair was in the next town to the east, a more active and populated town, and Owen was a midway ride operator. During this visit to the defunct diner, he was, fittingly, on his lunch hour.

The timeshares, which Owen's family, Dani's family, and countless others used during the summers by the lake, had moved to the other side of the town where the beaches were more suitable and commerce was more reliable.

"Two summers wasn't enough, was it?" Owen muttered.

That morning, Owen had sat on a stool next to the Ferris wheel controls and nursed a bag of popcorn. His mind had wandered to his summers at the timeshares, to the minutes and hours he had shared with Dani. Owen looked to other, faster rides only to get blurred views of short black hair like Dani's and laughter that he could replace with hers. All of these things he meant to distract him from the growing uncomfortable feeling he had inside.

Several times that morning, Owen had stood at the payphone and stared at a rippled slice of paper. He'd jotted a number he'd obtained with some research from the white pages. Dani Traxler's number. He could not think what to say to her over the phone. Instead, he thought about her tanned skin or her riding a bike down the dirt road, a smirk growing into a smile as she drew near to him. More daydreaming, more anxiety.

"Owen!" Martin, the supervising technician recalled Owen from his surreal world to the reality of the fair, the music and the elephant ears. "C'mon, pal. Break's over. There's a line forming."

"Think I remember us being here," Owen muttered, trying to picture Dani.

After a few long days, the fair would come to a close. It was autumn and there would be no further touring for the year. Owen had arranged for a related job elsewhere. He'd assumed, and perhaps hoped, his surge of emotion for Dani would pass as it had always done before. But this time, he found himself on the highway headed toward Markham, where his crumpled piece of paper dictated Dani's location. He wondered if she was still beautiful, if she was married or had children. He thought she would not be completely as he remembered her and tried furiously to imagine what person would be standing before him when he called upon her.

He tested possible verbal scenarios in the car.

"Hey! I was in the neighbourhood, and someone told me you…"

"Dani Traxler, long time no see huh?"

He smiled, and continued, feeling good about that introduction.

As he drove, he talked an hour or so away in an effort to anticipate any possible responses he might get. When he exited the highway, onto more local roads, he closely observed the parks and the restaurants and wondered if Dani visited any of these places or if she still liked to do the things they did together.

He stopped his car in the visitor's section of a semi-detached housing complex. Brown brick and shade from the trees planted long ago, Owen thought, made for a comfortable environment to pursue this most uncomfortable leap from normality. He listened for cicadas in the trees, like the ones near the lake, looked for a sign this was the right course of action. But it was out of season for cicadas; there was nothing to hear but the chirping of birds.

As if it was one motion, and not several, Owen walked through the winding streets looking for the address on his sheet of paper and, when he found it, without the hesitation he had demonstrated at the payphones, he knocked.

A moment of silence was rescued by the muffled sound of footsteps approaching the door. Then it opened. Fighting through nerves, Owen was at loss for words when he saw Dani who did not look entirely different at all.

"Oh. Hi," she said curiously, suggesting she suspected his visit was proof this was a small world.

"Hi." Owen allowed the word to barely escape his lips, and he looked back to where he'd walked from, and back again.

Unable to deal with the uncomfortable pause that followed, Dani remained silent. She had a curious nature but was baffled by the sight of Owen at her door. She tried to remember his name. Her mind raced through several possibilities and outright guesses. They had never officially met, but she remembered this quiet fellow with the distinct face from those summers she spent with family and friends at the timeshares up in the Kawartha Lakes district.

THREE-SIDED COIN
Shannon Moore

"Why, Doc? Can you answer that? What I'm asking you is why my life is an endless string of bad decisions, mistakes, and screw-ups? When am I ever going to catch a break? I guess that's what I really want to know. When will the shit storm subside, and let a little sunlight in?"

The good doctor tilted his head the way he always did when he was about to toss out some over-educated shrink bullshit. "Well, Chris, I think you're the only one who can truly answer that. Let me direct the question at you. When, Chris, will your life improve?"

He had been coming to see Doctor Manning for over a month now, and this was all he ever got. Re-directed questions that he was expected to answer. After an unsuccessful suicide attempt, Chris had decided it might be time to seek out a little help. A person who could show him that first breadcrumb, a guide. So far Doctor Manning hadn't been that person.

"What? No! You answer the damn question. What the hell am I paying you for? Answers, Doc. I am paying you for answers. Not more questions."

"Well, Chris, if I ask the right question, maybe you will have the answer. Subconsciously I think you know why your life hasn't been up to your idea of par lately."

"Of course I know why my life sucks. My question was, 'When is it going to get better?' Jesus! All those plaques on the wall, are they just for show?"

"No, Chris, they're..." the doctor's voice was cut off by the electronic beep of his timer. "Well, it looks like our time's up for today, Chris. So I guess we'll meet again next Wednesday."

"I don't know. I don't think were getting anywhere, and for the money I'm paying you I should know myself inside and out by now. And no offense, Doc, I don't know shit, and I don't think you do either. So I don't know. I might be here; I might not."

"Well, then, just make an appointment with Delores when you want to continue our sessions. And Chris, think about what I asked you today, okay?"

"Yeah, Doc."

He stood up from the comfortable leather chair, and headed into the waiting room. As he exited the small office he passed a young woman wearing a short skirt and carrying an umbrella. She walked with authority, but in a very graceful manner. Chris could not help but stare at her as she passed him. Noticing his eyes she shot him a small grin as she entered Doctor Manning's office.

"Wow!" he said after the door had fully closed. "Maybe today will be better?"

He took the elevator down to the first floor and steered towards the large glass doors that framed the busy street. Eyeing the Tim Horton's across the way, he began to make his way to the closest set of lights. During the day, this Tim Horton's location was packed with suits—lawyers, stock brokers, management types—all trying to get their coffee fix. In acid washed jeans, and a beat up leather jacket, Chris stood out like sore thumb.

"A large regular coffee, please."

"That will be $1.46 sir."

While handing the kid behind the counter a $10 bill, Chris glanced at his nametag. "Your father a big Johnny Cash fan?"

"What? I don't know. Why?"

"Well your name's Sue, like the Johnny Cash song. You know, 'My name is Sue, how do you do,' like the song."

"Ah, no. See that girl pouring your coffee, her name's Sue. I'm

Larry, I just thought it would be funny to change nametags for today. So far you're the only one to notice."

"Ah," was all Chris could say. How dumb had kids become.

"$8.54 is your change sir. Sorry about all the toonies. We ran out of $5 bills," Larry said as he handed over a handful of change and a large coffee.

"That's okay," Chris murmured as he turned to leave the crowded building.

"And sir…thanks for noticing my nametag."

"Yeah," Chris said as he pushed his way through the mass of navy suits. What an odd thing to say, he thought as he exited once again to the busy street.

The rain started in not two steps out of the Tim Horton's. Of course, he thought, the one day I don't bring an umbrella. He pulled the neck of his jacket up, and began to make his way through the storm.

Who gives a fuck what the little prick's name is, Davis thought as he stared at the man with the leather jacket. Why, when there's a line out the door, filled with people with real jobs, is this dumb prick making idle chitchat with the half-baked kid standing behind the counter?

Davis was by no means a large man; he was of average height, and average build, and a coward. His entire universe was himself. In his business life, he was cutthroat, unforgiving and hostile. Qualities prized in a good lawyer. In essence, Davis was a jackass.

Finally, the scruffy-looking man in the beat up leather jacket moved out of the way. How nice of you, Davis thought. Maybe you could have done that five goddamn minutes ago. We're not all on welfare, buddy. We don't have all the time in the world.

As he approached the counter, the greasy-faced Tim Horton's

worker gave Davis a welcoming smile. He took this to mean that the greasy faced Tim Horton's worker was in fact a homosexual trying to make some sort of sexual advance. Without looking him in the eye, Davis asked for a medium black coffee, the entire time thinking that if he looked him in the eye he would think he was gay. When his coffee finally came, Davis grabbed it, paid, and left the overcrowded Tim Horton's.

He only had a few more things to take care of at work, and then he was off to his favorite watering hole, Carol's. That would help him forget about this weird homosexual experience.

Davis walked through the giant black doors that hid Carol's from the rest of the world. Candy was on stage. Good, he thought to himself, it's the 'A' squad tonight, no ugly ones. As he sat down in the front row, he immediately started scanning the crowd for a waitress. After a few minutes of staring he finally got Rachel's attention.

"Same as always, Mr. Morrison?"

"Yeah, Rachel. Scotch on the rocks, like every other time," he said with what he thought was a seductive grin, but which, to Rachel, appeared more like the way villains smiled in old movies.

"Sure," she said, walking away from him. Davis's eyes followed her until she disappeared from sight. Damn, what I'd do to get inside that, he thought.

Candy finished, and the crowd was waiting for the next dancer to come on stage. Usually it was Daisy, but once in a while they would switch the order. Those were Davis's favorite nights, the ones he couldn't predict.

The speakers suddenly cracked and the DJ began speaking over the repetitive thump of bad dance music.

"Tonight, gentlemen, we have a real treat for you. We're about to introduce you to a brand new dancer. In fact, this is her first dance in front of a live crowd. Without further adieu, I would like you to meet Roxanne," the DJ screamed.

The smoke machines clicked on, and "Roxanne" by The Police started playing. A girl, no more then nineteen glided onto stage. She wore a schoolgirl uniform, modified of course, making it more revealing than the plaid skirts and white shirts tend to be. Since he had begun patronizing Carol's, Davis had never seen a stripper this beautiful. She had long flowing red hair and freckles that splashed her cheeks and spilled over her nose. He was mesmerized by the way she moved, deliberate, but without being rigid. She flowed around the stage the way a stream flows around rocks that obstruct its path. He had to have her. For the second time tonight he scanned the crowd for a waitress. They only tended to see him when his drink got low, so he downed his scotch and waited. After about five minutes of holding his empty glass in the air, Rachel came over to his side with a fresh scotch on her tray. As she placed the drink on the table in front of him and began to pull away, Davis caught her wrist.

"Hey, can you get me a private dance with her," Davis said and pointed at Roxanne.

"No, sweetie, she's too new. They won't let her do private dances for a couple of months."

"Well, how about this. It costs twenty bucks for a dance. What if I was willing to give her—hell, I don't know, how about two hundred? Would that maybe help change policy a bit?"

"I don't know, Mr. Morrison, it might? I'll have to ask my manager. Give me a second. I'll go get him." Rachel walked off, but this time Davis only had eyes for Roxanne who was just starting her second dance.

It took thirty minutes for the manager to make his way to where Davis was seated. He was dressed entirely in black, in contrast to his pale, almost pasty complexion. He was not a large man, but Davis knew from the way he carried himself he was not to be underestimated. Not physically or mentally.

"Mr. Morrison, is it? I came over to tell you that I can't allow Roxanne to accept your generous offer. But I can promise you one thing, when she's ready to give private dances, you will be her first. Does that work for you, Mr. Morrison?" the manager said, smiling politely as he finished speaking.

"Um, how about this. I give you three hundred dollars, and then I give Roxanne three hundred dollars for one dance, tonight? Does that help change your mind?"

The man in black looked at his feet for a second, appearing to debate this new offer. "I'll go talk to Roxanne. If she's okay with it, I'm okay with it. But I want you to give her the entire six hundred. I don't want any. I'll be back shortly. Have a drink on the house while you wait." He snapped his fingers and Rachel quickly brought another scotch on the rocks to Davis. The man in black nodded to no one in particular, then strode off in the direction of two big black doors that read "PRIVATE".

Davis was excited. The money meant nothing to him. It was much more important that he beat the system. He made six hundred dollars in an average consultation. He knew he had bought this girl. Money meant everything to these people, and that was the one thing that he had in large supply.

How greedy they are, Davis thought. For the right amount of money, I bet I could have convinced him to let me have a lap dance from his mother. What a weak prick.

After congratulating himself, Davis decided to turn his attention back to the stage. Daisy had just begun to strip down, his favorite part of the dance. When they actually took their clothes off. After they were naked the mystery was gone. That was not as exciting for Davis. He liked imagining what they looked like under what few clothes they wore. It was a game to him, and when the game finished what was the point of continuing to play.

A light tap on the shoulder stole his attention from the stage. Looking over his shoulder, he saw the wavy red hair and freckles that had so easily seduced him. Roxanne now wore what appeared to be a woman's business suit, but much shorter than the ones Davis was used to seeing. His entire body gyrated with excitement.

"I heard you're going to pay a lot of money to meet me in a more personal manner. It's nice to meet you, Mr. Morrison. I'm Roxanne, please follow me." She grabbed his hand and led him through the doorframe with a large glowing sign that read "V.I.P." in bold capital letters.

They walked down a long hallway lined with red velvet couches. Here and there a man sat with a naked woman straddling his lap. Davis could only recognize a few of the girls; the poor lighting made it very difficult to see much at all.

When they finally arrived at their spot, Roxanne pushed Davis into the seat. "My manager told me you offered six hundred dollars for a dance with me? I'm flattered but, before we start, I want you to know that this is only a dance, nothing more. No touching and no extras."

"Fine, fine, no touching, no extras. Got it."

"Also, I'd like the money up front. If you could do that for me, I'll give you two dances instead of one, deal?"

Davis reached into his pants and pulled out his wallet. He flipped it open and began counting out loud. "One hundred, two hundred, three hundred…" He continued to six hundred. When he reached it, he flipped his wallet closed and shoved it back into his pocket. Then he handed Roxanne her money.

"Thanks," she said as she placed the money in her purse. Then she sat on Davis lap and began moving provocatively, taking off her shirt and bra in the process.

Slowly, Davis moved his hands over her exposed breasts.

"No, sweetie, remember what we talked about," Roxanne purred as she removed his hands.

She stood up, took off the bottom half of her outfit, and once again slowly lowered herself to Davis's lap. Not a minute passed before Davis's hands were once again moving to touch what he had been warned was forbidden, the entire time thinking, I paid six hundred dollars for this; for the next two songs I own this little tramp.

Finally, Roxanne stopped moving and turned to face Davis. "That's it, Mr. Morrison, your time is up!" she said as she got off his lap.

"No, you said two songs. We haven't even got through one yet. You're not going anywhere with my six hundred until you do what I paid you to do. So, sit the fuck back down."

"John," she screamed. "We have a problem."

At that, a very large man in black pants and a black t-shirt with the word "SECURITY" on it came running. Without asking what the problem was, he grabbed Davis by the front of his shirt and hauled him out of his seat.

"Don't fucking touch me, you dumb prick. Do you know who the fuck I am? What you're doing right now is assault, and I have the power to crush you like the dumb fuck you are!" Davis screamed as he was dragged though a door and into what looked like a change room.

"Is that right, buddy? Wait till we get outside, then we'll see who's crushing whom," the bouncer said as he threw Davis through an open door into the pouring rain. He landed on his back on the wet concrete, his head smashing against the ground. For a moment the world went black, then he was being lifted off the ground. Behind the large bouncer, Davis could see more dark shapes spilling out of the open strip club door. Something hit his face, and once again he was on the ground. This time no one picked him up. Instead, more feet than Davis could count began slamming into his body. Once again the world went black, this time for much longer than a moment.

When Davis awoke he found himself lying behind a dumpster in an alley. His body pulsed with pain. His head swam and he immediately threw up. When he regained his composure, he noticed that his jacket, wallet and shoes were missing. He could see nothing out of his left eye.

Tears rolled down his bruised cheeks. "What am I going to tell Debby?" he said out loud. "She's going to take everything. Oh God, what have I done?" Davis placed a hand on the rusty dumpster and began to stand. The tears continued, but no one would have noticed with the rain coming down so hard. He stumbled off down the alley clutching his ribs, the storm raging around him.

She couldn't cry. Not in front of the customers. She had to contain herself. It was already two-forty, and she was allowed to go home at three. That's when her shift ended and she could get back to Timothy. Rita had called earlier and said that she had put him to bed around nine and that he went down easily. She called again around eleven and said that the storm had woken him up and that she would try her best to get him back to sleep. She hadn't spoken to Rita since; she had been on stage most of the night, being Roxanne.

The feeling of that disgusting little man's hands all over her was haunting. She had told them she wasn't ready, and they had agreed...until Scott informed her that the man was willing to pay six hundred dollars, which changed her tune. Miranda didn't know what sickened her more: Mr. Morrison or her own greed. She didn't think it was possible that her opinion of herself could drop any lower than it already was. She was a stripper, a fucking stripper. From the honour roll in high school to the University of Toronto to this. She sickened herself. If her family knew, they would probably disown her.

Timothy was only fourteen months old. She had gotten pregnant in her first year of university. An abortion was out of the question. Her family would have really disowned her. She could still hear her father's voice, "We're Catholic, the whole street's Catholic. What would the neighbours think? No, it's out of the question. You will own up to your mistakes, and deal with the consequences, so help me God." So now she spent her days going to class, her evenings studying and being as much as of a mother as she could, and her nights…well, that was what she hated about herself. And this was only her first real shift; she could already tell it wasn't going to get better.

"You can go home darling." She turned to find Scott standing behind her. "You did good, you know. John said the guy was being belligerent, basically saying he owned you or something, I don't know. Well, no need to worry. He won't be allowed back in here."

"Thanks, Scott. I'm sorry I panicked. It's just that his hands, his sweaty hands were… it won't happen again, I promise."

"It wasn't your fault. You did what needed to be done. Believe me, he would have tried again. I know the type; he had no plans to stop. You could have told him until you were blue in the face, and he would have done exactly what he wanted. Rich people, you know."

"Yeah, thanks," Miranda said as she brushed tears off her cheek. When did I start crying? she thought.

"But I'm not going to let you do any more lap dances for a while. I said you weren't ready and I meant that."

"Okay. How was my dancing by the way?"

"Oh, baby, that was incredible. I knew I would have no problem starting you off on my 'A' squad. You're a natural."

"Thanks, Scott," Miranda mumbled as her cheeks reddened with embarrassment. Standing, she turned her back to Scott and began packing up her things.

"One more thing, kiddo. Before you go, you may want to give John about one hundred bucks of that money. He saved you tonight. If you want him to be that fast in the future, you gotta keep him happy. Okay? Now go get yourself a coffee." With this Scott turned and headed out of the change room.

Miranda had forgotten that it was expected the talent would tip the bouncers when they helped them out. She quickly finished packing up her stuff and went in search of John.

She found him sitting at the bar talking to Kim, the head bartender.

"Um, John. This is for you. Thanks for helping me out tonight," Miranda said as she handed him one hundred and fifty dollars, more than Scott had recommended.

"What? No, Miranda," John said as he pushed the money back at her. "You don't have to tip me for doing my job. Anyways, I've been trying to find a reason to kick that little prick's ass since he tried to follow Rachel home one night. Thanks, but no thanks. It was my pleasure."

"Are you sure? You know he gave me six hundred, right?"

"Yeah, I know. But rumour has it you have a kid at home. So how about you take the money you were going to give me and buy him a football or something. Deal?"

"Deal," Miranda said, as a giant smile formed on her face.

She left Carol's the back way. The 'talent door' it was called. She decided that Scott was right. She really needed coffee. Tim Horton's wasn't too far away so she decided to walk; she would come back for her car after her coffee.

When she arrived, a girl named Larry served her. She looked very tired, so Miranda didn't bother asking how she came to have such a peculiar name for a girl. Her extra-large double-double came quicker than she expected. Grabbing it off the counter, she took the closest empty seat.

Miranda knew this area very well. Not only did she work and live nearby but her therapist was in the building right across the street from the very Tim Horton's she now sat in. Rita said it was dumb that she went to see a shrink, but Miranda didn't care. Doctor Manning was helping her through a lot of her problems. And the money didn't matter; her grandmother paid for it. She said it would be good for her to know herself better now that she was a mother. Next Wednesday she had another appointment; it fell between two classes so it didn't really affect her day much. I wonder if I should bring up tonight at my next session, she thought.

All of a sudden the night's events came flooding back. The feel of the man's clammy hands caressing her body sent shivers down her spine. She didn't feel much like finishing her coffee. She stood, grabbed her umbrella, and headed out the door into the storm leaving her cup on the table for Larry to clean up.

Why had he decided to come back? Doctor Manning was an idiot. Another session of nothing but questions, mostly his own directed back at him. Answers…when would he start getting answers? Chris pushed the elevator button. He was hoping to see the good-looking girl from last Wednesday, but no such luck. He had promised himself that if he saw her again he would ask her to coffee. But, God seemed to hate him. So he probably wouldn't see the girl ever again. The doors of the elevator opened and he stepped in.

She's going to ruin my life. I don't think so. That dumb bitch says she'll take me for everything I've got, just for going to a strip club a couple of nights a week. "I don't think so," Davis said out loud as he hammered on the elevator button. His ribs still hurt from where the bouncers had kicked him. The doctor told him three were broken and a few more were bruised. The doctor also told him to take a few days off but going home was hell. Work felt better. Well, that was until today. They'd served him the papers just a few minutes ago. He was fucked. Being a lawyer, Davis could smell an open and shut case. If his wife added this to all the abuse and the many affairs he'd had, she could easily take him for everything. He was fucked but he wasn't going to be stuck. Nope, he'd die before he saw that bitch get a goddamn penny.

Finally, the door to the elevator opened to a scruffy man in a leather jacket.

"Is this going up?" Davis asked even though he already saw the giant illuminated arrow pointing down.

"Nope," the man in the leather jacket replied.

Davis let the door shut and looked at the elevator buttons. In his rush to get to the roof, he must have pressed the "Down" button. Well, this time he'd get it right. "She's going to regret ever threatening me," Davis said as he furiously pressed the "Up" button.

As she stepped into the large grey building that housed Doctor Manning's office, Miranda noticed a man moving in her direction. He was good looking, although a little scruffy, and he appeared to be a few years older than she was. The man was large, but in no way could he be considered fat, just bigger than average. He wore a beat up leather jacket, and blue jeans. He looked out of place. As soon as he got close to her, he stopped and began rubbing his head in an almost nervous fashion.

"Um...Miss, you don't know me, but my name is Chris. I don't know if you remember, but we passed in the hall last Wednesday."

"Yes, I remember," she said, even though she didn't. "My name is Miranda."

She stuck out her hand, and he grasped it lightly.

"Hi, I'm Chris. Shit, I already said that didn't I?"

Miranda nodded, grinning at how shy this man was.

"Yeah, I thought so. It's just you're so good looking I can't seem to concentrate. Anyways, I don't mean to be forward, but I promised myself that if I ever saw you again I would ask you out for a coffee. So...um...would you like to get coffee sometime?"

"Sure, that would be nice," Miranda said while pulling a pad of paper out of her purse. "How about I give you my number." She wrote on the small piece of paper and handed it to him.

"Thanks. I'll give you a call and we can arrange a time you aren't too busy. Nice meeting you." With that Chris turned and headed towards the giant glass doors that led to the busy street.

"Wait," Miranda called after him. "What are you doing in an hour?"

Chris turned to face her, still rubbing his head nervously. "Nothing. Why?"

"Well, after my appointment, maybe we can get some coffee, if you don't mind waiting, that is?"

"No, I don't mind. I'll just go shopping for an hour and meet you back here in the lobby."

"That would be great," Miranda said. Chris gave a short wave and once again turned towards the door.

"Wait," Miranda called out again. Now it was her turn to be nervous. "I have a son."

Chris turned and looked at her with a puzzled expression. "I have a dog. What's your point?"

Miranda could only smile.

"One regular coffee and one butter tart. Is that correct?"

"Yep, that's right," the customer replied.

"Okay, that'll be $2.87," Larry answered. He hated working in the day; the dumb suits came in and acted all high and mighty. Man, did it piss him off. He looked back at Sue, she caught his eye and stuck her tongue out in response. Larry hadn't worked up the nerve to ask her out yet, but today felt like as good a time as any.

Sue handed Larry the man's coffee and the little brown bag that contained his butter tart. Before the man's hand closed around the coffee cup, a crash came from outside. So loud that it caused Larry to drop the coffee cup, which hit the counter and spilled its contents on the floor.

"I am so sorry," Larry apologized, but the man wasn't paying any attention. He was staring out the window looking at the source of the crash. "What is it? An accident?"

"No, it was a man," another customer said without averting his eyes from the big plate glass window.

"Someone hit a man?" Larry replied, confused about what had actually happened.

"No, it looks like he jumped. Oh my God! Don't look, kid. It's not pretty."

"Jesus," was all Larry could say.

The customer looked back at Larry, first glancing at his chest.

"Sue? Was your Dad a Johnny Cash fan?"

VANITY
Ashley Rae Smith

In a kitchen, a sink full of dishes lay dirty, the victims of days upon days of neglect. A faint smell of what could be described as decaying garbage rose from the floor.

This kitchen was the same as almost every other room in the house: white. The only exception was the main room that contained a full-length mirror and a green chair. There, a beautiful young woman sat, slumped in the green chair, looking into the full-length mirror.

"I remember when I was a child. Sally and I used to play Princess and the Maid by the pond. I used to be the maid and Sally the Princess. Sally told me that we'd be friends forever and the pond would be our secret fortress. I often wondered what it would be like if I had to drown her in that pond that she loved so very much."

The thought brought a smile to the young woman's face, not a happy smile but a wicked one.

"It's not that I hated Sally, she was just a stupid little girl of no consequence."

The image in the mirror flickered.

"Oh, don't give me that look, that judgmental look. You didn't understand Sally. She was beautiful on the outside but ugly on the inside. I was the only one who could see that. Sally was nobody, yet she was loved by everyone, whereas I fell into the shadows, noticed by no one."

The image flickered again.

The young woman became angry and stood up from her chair. "I don't have to take this!" she said as she left the room.

* * *

When the young woman returned to the room, she seemed to have aged. She sat down in the green chair and once again looked at the image across from her…in the mirror.

"You know that Sally was a blonde. Her hair was to her waist, with ringlets. She used to wear long, white lacey dresses. She liked to twirl. Her hair used to sway back and forth. It drove the boys crazy. Oh how she loved to drive the boys crazy."

The woman got up from her chair and went to the kitchen. When she came back, she was holding a pair of kitchen shears and a towel.

"You know what I did to Sally?" she asked the image as she took the shears to her hair. "I chopped off all Sally's hair while she slept, leaving only blood where I cut too deeply."

As her hair fell to the ground, the woman found herself growing tried. But she ignored the sleep that pressed on her and continued to stare directly into the image that confronted her.

"Sally was a witch. She deserved what she got."

A cold stare came back from the image.

"You don't believe me that she was wicked and deserved it? You'll soon see and understand my pain," the woman said bitterly.

The image in the mirror appeared to be laughing. It pointed its finger. The woman stifled a slight sob as she wept into the arm of the green chair.

"What could you know about my pain?" She banged her fists into the arms of the green chair. In the shadows, her face seemed creased. "Don't you dare judge me!"

After a few minutes of heavy sobbing, the woman was able to compose herself.

"Sorry, I didn't mean to lose control like that. I just get a little crazy when I haven't taken my meds."

As reached over for the pills and popped them into her

mouth, the large scars where she had dug deeply into her own flesh became visible.

"One time Sally was playing hop scotch. She would throw the rock and jump to wherever it fell. But she threw the rock too far and fell hard on her knees, scraping them badly. I remember the blood flowing down her leg, red blood everywhere."

The thought of this made the woman lick her lips as if she were savoring the taste of Sally's blood.

"And do you think that she cried? Oh no! That little witch just sat and laughed as if to spite me, to take away my one moment in the sun!" the woman screamed. She stood up quickly. "Why don't you understand what I'm trying to say to you?" she said as her arms hit the side of her body. Then she fell back into the green chair.

"I bet you feel pity for me?" The woman asked the image. "Don't! I don't need your sympathy. All I need is your understanding," she cried out, almost in tears. She leaned forward in her chair, towards the mirror, and grabbed more of the pills from the table. She threw them into her mouth. Calming herself, she leaned back in her chair.

"Sally used to have this doll. It was her favorite. She took that doll everywhere. She would tell it stories about herself and about the people in her life. She would sing to it and love it like it were her child."

The woman sighed before continuing.

"Oh how she loved that doll. It made her so happy. Of course her happiness could not be tolerated!"

The image in the mirror replied, "What did you do to Sally's doll?"

The woman looked at the image smugly and said, "One night while Sally was sleeping I stole the doll, made a little camp fire, and burned it to a crisp. I watched happily as it started to melt. It was like watching Sally's innocence burn away. The next day Sally realized her doll was missing. Did she cry? Did she feel any remorse for her missing doll? Did she miss missing her innocence? Oh no, not Sally. She just picked up a new doll and made it her favourite. The snotty girl didn't even care enough to cry a little about the doll that she apparently loved so much. She could pick up something fast and then forget about it soon after."

The image in the mirror appeared to smirk. "Oh, you must have suffered, all your pain and anger...all for nothing."

The woman sat up in her chair, pointed at the reflection in the mirror and shouted: "Don't you dare mock me!" Then she fell back into the chair, tired from the exhaustion that had poisoned her mind and body.

* * *

The woman appeared to have aged considerably. She had gained the distinguished lines of a woman who had lived her entire life lonely and bitter. Her skin was like rawhide, sizzled bacon. She looked as though she had been out in the sun far too long.

"You know, you're probably one of the few friends I have who understands me."

The image only flickered to show acknowledgement.

"I remember when Sally and I entered a beauty pageant. Sally came in first. She was always considered beautiful and graceful. I came in second. Oh, how Sally walked up and down, strutting in front of all the spectators."

The woman rubbed her hands together.

The image in the mirror interrupted: "This makes you happy? And here I thought that you hated Sally?"

The woman chuckled to herself wickedly and then replied: "Oh, don't get me wrong. Watching Sally walking up and down sent chills through my soul. But what happened next made my heart skip a beat. As Sally was making her final round, her dress got caught in the heel of her shoe. Her strapless dress fell, exposing her naked, ugly body for the whole world to see. Sally was humiliated and she cried in the change room."

The face in the mirror became concerned. "Poor Sally, she must have been devastated!"

The smirk on the woman's lips widened, revealing deep lines in her face. Bags emerged beneath her dark eyes.

"Of course! I went to see how Sally was. She was crying. So I comforted her. As the tears fell down her face, I took one onto my finger and placed my finger in my mouth. As I savoured the taste of it, I thought, 'So, this what Sally's humiliation tastes like?' I liked it; I liked the thought of Sally's weakness." The woman licked her lips. "I liked the taste of Sally's humiliation. It gave me great pleasure." The woman wanted to stand up, triumphant, but she was too weak, too tired to even bother trying. Her body was failing her. Her skin sagged. Her face drooped. She was nothing more than skin and bones, too depleted to talk or move, although the image in the mirror appeared to have had become young and more vibrant looking. With her last ounce of strength, the woman lifted her hand and pointed at the image as if to speak, but her arm fell with her eyelids and there, in her green chair, she slept the sleep of the ages.

REPERCUSSIONS
Dylan Inksetter

"I don't like that we allowed the situation to get so out of control."

"Neither do I, but obviously there isn't any point in wishing for the situation to be any different. It is the way it is, and now we have to deal with it." A silence stretched as the two figures stared straight ahead, pondering the implications of this meeting and what it would set into motion.

They were each seated in elegant leather lounge chairs facing a flickering fireplace, the sole source of light in the room. The small bluish flames from the fire in front of them caused shadows to leap around the walls, as if caught in perpetual flight from some unseen pursuer. A well-crafted wooden side table was positioned between the two chairs. The items on the table seemed to be placed as if to mirror the room around it. Two glasses stood opposite each other, both filled with red liquid. They were facing a tall twisted bottle that glowed with the light of the fire. Between the glasses were two sheets of papers, one on top of the other. A gloved hand reached out and lifted one glass, removing it from the scene. The table now seemed unbalanced and somewhat empty.

"What do your instincts tell you to do?" one figure asked.

After a slight pause, the other replied, "You know my feelings on the matter. I believe that we must take preventive action to ensure our own safety."

"Do you truly believe they pose a danger to us?"

Another pause.

"No. Not yet. But they are exhibiting all the signs of an emerging danger. If we delay then they will undoubtedly be recruited by our adversaries."

"You are dealing with maybes and ifs. It would be a shame to attack a nation on possibilities alone."

"I know all this. I have given as much thought to it as you have."

"I realize that and I must admit that I agree with your conclusion. But let us pretend, for argument's sake, that I disagree. Go through your reasoning process, and I will attempt to dissuade you."

"Very well." The figure twirled his glass, causing the liquid inside to release a fruity fragrance into the air for the briefest of moments. "Let us start small and work our way up."

"As you wish."

"First of all, we must look at their social structure. They are basically savages. They are infested with greed, crime, and disorder. And they are divided into factions which constantly struggle and scheme against each other. This has reduced them to little more than warring brutes whose philosophy is survival of the fittest. They don't even view all of their own people as equals."

"Perhaps if we were to show them the error of their ways they would unite and thrive under our guidance."

"Oh, they would unite. But they would unite against us as a common enemy."

"Which would force us to act anyway?"

"Precisely. In addition, their leaders are not to be trusted. They are either the aristocratic elite and wealthy who look after only themselves, or militaristic warlords who also look after only themselves."

"They cannot all be classified under those two headings."

"No, I admit that there would be a few with whom we could probably reason, but they would be drowned out by the multitude."

"But it has not necessarily been the people's choice to be ruled as they are."

"They allowed it to happen, and continue to allow themselves to be abused. You know, as well as I, that it is the *people* who have the true power in any system, and the *people* who dictate how a system evolves."

"True, but they are still in the evolutionary stage. They may yet change their ways."

"No. I assure you that they will not. They have backed themselves into a corner that has forced them into their current state of chaos and fear. There is no way out for them without warfare which would, in the end, put them right back where they are now."

"I must agree. Could we not then force them to co-operate with our wishes? We could easily overpower their military and install our own leaders."

"We could, but they would hate us for it, and the hatred would remain. They would eventually rebel and view it as fighting for their freedom."

"We would also lose some of our own soldiers, no matter how superior we are."

"Which is why we must strike now, from a distance."

"It seems unfair to strike at them while we sit safely out of reach."

"We are only out of their reach for the moment. Give them fifty or a hundred years, and they will be at the point where they could strike at us. At such time they will, without a doubt, be contacted by our rivals."

"What about diplomatic missions of our own at that time? Could we not convince them to join with us instead?"

"I wish it were that easy. They do not look kindly on outsiders; they don't even trust each other. The chances of a successful diplomatic mission are very slim. Even finding a diplomat willing to take on the mission will be difficult. You, yourself, asked for volunteers years ago, but no one wanted to go."

"Why are they are so feared?"

"Because they are so violent, another reason why diplomacy would be doomed from the start. Their past tells it all. Throughout their history they have consistently warred with friends and neighbours. They are not exactly good at honouring agreements. They will be more than happy to bite the hand that feeds them as soon as they are able. They thrive on struggle."

"That, I believe, is the key."

"That they thrive on struggle?"

"Yes. It is that which most frightens me. In that sense, they truly do resemble our enemies."

The two figures sat in silence for a while.

"Look at it this way."

"I'm listening."

"Suppose we send diplomats, the talks go well, and we become friends."

"Yes, go on."

"They would want our technologies, and one way or another they would eventually get them. Either we would provide the technology to them, or their own scientists would be inspired to develop technologies of equal sophistication. Even if they stay friends with us, would you trust them with our weapons?"

"Ha! Not likely. I wouldn't trust them with half our knowledge."

"It would be like, pardon the phrase, 'trusting a weasel to guard the hens', would it not?"

"True."

"Are we agreed then?"

"Sadly, yes."

After a few moments of quiet deliberation, the figure on the left reached for one of the two sheets of paper lying on the table between their two chairs. He signed his name to the bottom then handed the sheet to his companion. The other he took up and tossed unceremoniously into the fire. The fragile paper held out for a second, but then the fire caught it, and it was consumed. The room was illuminated briefly and then returned to an almost deeper darkness as the fire resumed its original happy flickering.

The figure on the right then pressed a button on the arm of his chair and a part of the wall slid open, revealing a starry sky beyond thick glass.

"You knew the outcome of these talks before we started."

"I did. I wanted to convince myself otherwise, but I knew how this would end."

"We didn't even talk about resources or consumption."

"I know."

"It was simply a question of destroying them now, or destroying them later. You realize that?"

"Yes, but I am still saddened by it."

"As am I."

A door opened behind the two seated figures and a third individual cautiously entered the room. "You have reached a decision?"

"Yes. You have a green light."

"I am sorry to hear that," said the intruder.

"We know, but we firmly believe the decision to be the correct choice of action. Has the brain finished cataloguing the information?"

"Right back to the very beginning. All we need is a final classification."

"Entitle it 'Earth 6.2.1'."

"Very well." The figure bowed, reached for the sheet with the signatures, and then left the room.

The seated figures remained silent, watching, as their room rotated. Finally, a small blue dot became visible through the glass, alone in the distant expanse of dark space. They examined it for a minute or two and, then, with a sigh, the one on the right pressed the button on his chair again. The wall slid shut, and the blue dot disappeared.

"I really enjoyed their wine though."

"Yes, it is what I will miss the most."

THE TRIBE
Dan Cox

Dorian Mitchell, March 18th, 1946: Day 3

It has been three days since we crashed. Our plane was on route to Brazil to assist some farmers there. We had heard they were enduring a terrible drought. A sudden storm took our plane down. Luckily, we landed near an island; otherwise, we would never have survived in the cold water. Sixteen people were on the flight from New York to Brazil; Lynn Holdsworth, Isaac Dull, Christobel Focell, and I were the only ones that we know of to make it to the island.

Isaac came on the trip because of his family. Before the drought, some of his relatives had moved to Brazil to farm and he hoped to assist them. Christobel won't say much about his past; he's been quiet ever since we met. Lynn has been doing this kind of thing for years, it seems, going to exotic places and helping people. She seems like a bit of a weird one to me.

I served my country against the Nazis. When I was shot in the arm, they sent me back home. But after three years away, my girl had given up hope of ever seeing me again and moved on. So I had come to Brazil to clear my head and do something good with my life.

Even though we're trapped here, the island is certainly something to behold. White sandy beaches and a bright blue, cloudless sky surrounds us. Further inland there's a vast jungle. This certainly LOOKS like South America, but I can't tell if we're anywhere near Brazil. That doesn't really matter now though. What matters now is surviving until we're rescued.

So far, we've been able to manage not too badly. Quite a lot of what we had on the plane has washed up on shore. We're sure there must be more elsewhere but we've been too busy making sure everyone is okay to venture into the jungle or explore the shore. Lynn has suggested we check the island tomorrow for any other signs of life. So, tomorrow we will search for more supplies and see if there is anyone else on this island.

March 19th, 1946: Day 4

It appears there IS human life on this island! When we couldn't find any more supplies, we ventured into the jungle. After about an hour of wandering, we stumbled upon a large village of natives. But I do wish that we'd run into a different tribe. These people are certainly strange. They adorn themselves with various animal bones and have extremely peculiar markings on their faces; these look far too similar to human skulls for my liking. They appear to be peaceful, however. When they first saw us they were ambivalent. But it didn't take long for them to warm up to Lynn and then begin to believe that we meant no harm.

Isaac doesn't like them. He goes on about how they creep him out. It would be better if I could silence him but I don't completely disagree with his view. They seem peaceful enough but those markings disturb the hell out of me. Why do they look so much like damned skulls? Christobel thinks they might be cannibals, but then why the animal bones?

I can't figure this out tonight. Lynn has been chatting with the tribe quite a bit, trying to learn something of their language. Maybe she can tell us something in the morning. Isaac, Chris, and I will be sleeping on the shore again tonight. We still aren't sure about the natives. However, Lynn seems to think they're safe, so she'll be staying in their village.

Lynn Holdsworth, Four Days after the Crash

I've taken a few pages from Dorian's journal. I'm going to keep a journal of my own. This situation is far too interesting to not record on paper. I hope he doesn't mind my stealing his pages. Though I doubt he'll even notice.

It's been what I can only assume to be four days after our crash landing and we've already managed to meet the locals! They're a sweet people. They seemed nervous at first; they'd probably never encountered white people before. Once I showed them we weren't to be feared, they brightened up and were terribly curious about who we were. These people are obviously quite bright. Their huts are built at the base of trees, and I can only assume this is to give the houses extra support. They intrigue me to no end; I hope I can learn as much as possible from them.

The boys don't seem to share my enthusiasm. They were too scared to stay in the village overnight. So I guess I'll have to be the "brave" one and find out for myself! Men can be so ridiculous sometimes.

March 20th, 1946: Day 5

Lynn came back this morning from the village. She had the same markings on her face as those villagers! There's no doubt in my mind now they're skulls. Lynn disagrees, of course, but there's nothing else that they COULD be. I hoped deep down inside that Lynn was right. But, when we got to the village later in the morning, I felt more and more disturbed.

As we entered the village, the people seemed less "kind". They stared at us more and looked contemptuous; it was terribly eerie. They set up a large meal for all of us and they seemed to get angry if we stopped eating. At this point I KNEW what was going on. They were trying to fatten us up. The food they served was animal, but none of the natives ate anything.

I talked with the other men and we all agree. Lynn got angry when we suggested the idea. She started yelling at us. She denied they would do something like that. But there's no other explanation. Neither myself nor the other men have ever seen those people eat anything. After the discussion, Lynn stopped talking to us and went back to the village.

Six Days after the Crash

The people here have been SO kind! I can't believe all the things I've learned about their culture. The boys didn't seem to like the fact that I let the villagers put their tribal markings on me. They're scared because they look like skulls. But they won't listen when I tell them that skulls don't mean the same thing to these people that they do to us. Skulls here are a sign of humanity. No matter how a person looks on the outside, we're all essentially the same on the inside. However the boys just think it must mean "poison" or something. They even suggested that the people are cannibals! They asked why they've never seen the "natives" eat. I told them it's because of respect, but they were so busy yelling over each other about what to do that I don't even think they heard me. After that I just left. There was no point in arguing with them. They can't be angry at these people for long. Soon they'll realize these people mean no harm.

I'm curious about Christobel; he didn't say much through the whole ordeal. Maybe he sees things the way I do.

Seven Days after the Crash

Christobel is a fucking asshole! Tonight, he came to the village alone. It was quite late, but I hoped he was beginning to understand that these people are not to be feared. He said he didn't want to sleep on the shore anymore and wished to stay here overnight. So the villagers gave him a room. Not long into the night, I heard a scream from one of the huts. When I got there, I saw that Christobel was trying to have his way with one of the women! I couldn't believe it! These people have been so generous to us and he tried to do THAT! The villagers wouldn't have it. When they tried to escort him out of the village to his camp, he attacked them! I won't be surprised if something happens to him. He deserves whatever he gets.

March 24th, 1946: Day 9

It's been getting stranger here since the last time I wrote in this journal. Chris has been missing for two days now. I'm positive the savages took him. He was the biggest of us but not the strongest. The morning he went missing, Isaac asked Lynn if the natives had anything to do with it. Lynn looked unsurprised at the news of Chris's disappearance. She said he deserved whatever he got! What did he "get"? How does she know anything about it? I realized that she must've been tricked by the savages. Isaac asked her if she knew what happened to Chris. She paused and said arrogantly that she had no idea. Ever since then she hasn't spoken to us. She's always at the village now. The villagers leave food for us at our camp, fatty foods, nothing lean. We won't go to their village; it's too dangerous. Last we saw, they had spears. They didn't have spears before.

Nine Days after the Crash

Dorian and Isaac have been acting bizarre the last two days. They've been sneaking around the outskirts of the village and looking angry. So I confronted them. When I did, they accused the tribe of killing Christobel. I couldn't take it and told them what I felt. This was not the best choice, however, since it sent them into a fit of rage. I tried to explain what he did and what happened but they wouldn't listen. After I finished explaining, Isaac hit me and said that I must know what happened to him. I couldn't believe he would hit me, after I had just told him what he wanted to know.

I shouldn't have said anything, but I didn't know how to react. They're just going crazy. The men in the village are worried about what the boys might do. So I suggested they arm themselves more. Just to be safe.

Although Dorian and Isaac won't come into the village any more, I asked the villagers to leave food for them at their camp so they don't starve. I hope they're eating it.

Tonight, we found Christobel's body; the villagers think he was killed by a jaguar. The tribe has agreed that we should send some people to guard Dorian and Isaac at night. They don't know how to protect themselves.

March 27th, 1946: Day 12

The brutes have been stalking us! I've woken up on occasion and seen them sneaking around our camp with spears! Once they notice that I've seen them, they run off. I swear to God they're trying to kill us.

I haven't seen Lynn since the last time I wrote in here. Isaac hasn't seen her either and he's getting scared. He doesn't want to die in his sleep and end up a meal for another man.

We've decided that we're going to keep watch at night. Take shifts and make sure they don't get too near. We must survive. Planes have been flying overhead occasionally. People must be looking for us. But they don't see our signals in the sand. With luck, one of the next planes will see our new, larger ones.

March 29th, 1946: Day 14

More planes have passed and not a single one has seen us. I now wonder if they were even looking for us. Isaac has already given up hope.

The savages look to be getting anxious. They come at night, but only briefly. And once they see that we're awake, they sneak away again. However, it's not long before they come back again. Obviously waiting for the moment where we let our guard down. Thankfully, neither of us have done so, but we will have to do something soon before they become too bold.

Fourteen Days after the Crash

Oh my, it's been quite some time since I've written. The boys seem to be managing well, although they do scowl more than usual and won't come into the village at all. But they seem to be safe.

Life in the village has been fantastic though! I doubt the boys even recognize me now. I've gotten so tanned and dirty from living in the huts. I've learned to hunt too. It's an amazing experience being here. I just wish the boys would realize what they're missing. I don't want them to end up like Christobel; no matter how much of an asshole he was, he really didn't deserve what he got.

March 30th, 1946: Day 15

I found Chris. His shoe anyway, as well as dried blood near it. And what's more? It was not two yards from the village! Isaac is terrified and so am I. We need better weapons. We've made spears for hunting as we cannot trust the food the savages give us anymore. But the villagers' spears are much more lethal and they're much more skilled with them.

Isaac has managed to find more supplies along the shore. We wonder now how much more may have drifted in since we last checked.

March 31st, 1946: Day 16

Thank God. After searching the shore for supplies, we found one crate that carried weapons, rifles to be exact. Ammo too. Those bloody savages are going to pay for what they've done to Chris and Lynn.

We will attack right before nightfall, before they send their hunters to our camp.

Sixteen Days after the Crash

Oh God! They have guns. I was collecting fruit near the shore when I saw them. They found a crate of guns. I overheard them talking to each other about an "attack" and saying "bloody savages". I came back to the village and told the people we should evacuate, even if it's temporary. They disagreed. This is their home; they've lived here for generations and won't leave. They believe a peaceful resolution can be accomplished. I hope they're right.

Either way I can't sleep. I hope the boys realize what they're doing.

April 2nd, 1946: Day 18

We did it.

We killed those bastard savages before they could get to us. Although they were prepared for us, they didn't stand a chance against American ingenuity. Bloody savages got me pretty good though. The bleeding has slowed, but I don't know how long I've got. At least Isaac will survive. He's a good man with a loving family. I'm older; I've lived well and served my country and its clearly time for me to go. Isaac has gotten pretty handy with making signal fires now. He should be able get a good smoke signal going and get out of here.

April 2nd, 1946: Day 19

The smell of rotting flesh has become more than we can bear. And animals have been driven here by that same smell. Thankfully, they've been more absorbed in eating the dead than chasing us. But I'm bleeding and, without a doubt, they'll come for me next. Then Isaac, If someone doesn't save us soon. I don't think I'll survive the night, though. There are too many beasts out there. Isaac will run out of ammo soon, too. I hope to God someone can find us in time.

THE SWALLOW
Claudia Cion

It took him only a few seconds to fall from the balcony and hit the ground. In an instant, pain owned every part of his body, erasing memories from his mind. Lying on his left side, Andrei breathed the agony of his last minutes. Death refused to come right away but revealed its presence to him slowly, like springtime reluctant to fold into summer.

On that plain evening, tragedy blocked the pulse of the neighbourhood. Mothers waiting for their children to arrive home from school took furtive glimpses from their windows, from their balconies. From safe spots on the sidewalk, others, walking home from their daily business, peered. One after another, they could not believe their eyes: a young man in pajamas lying in the building's garden. They were very confused when they recognized their long-time neighbour, the victim and the culprit. All together, suddenly, they forgot what they were on route to do, only to watch Andrei, flesh and blood, in the middle of the green space.

After moments of consternation, whispers began turning into screams.

"What happened?"

"What he is doing there?"

"Is he drunk?"

"Is he sick?"

"Is he, oh my God...?"

"Somebody call the superintendent!"

"Where is the superintendent?"

Panicked, nobody realized that the superintendent was among them. He had run from his office upon hearing the first screams. Under pressure from the group, he stepped out from the growing crowd and approached Andrei. He stared at his pale face, the embodiment of an impressionist painting. Andrei moved slowly and the damp land showed the mark of his body, the witness to his fall. He was groaning in pain.

Terrified, the superintendent asked foolishly, "What happened?"

With unaltered consciousness, Andrei answered, "I jumped."

The thirst of curiosity governed common sense and, as an antagonist would, pushed the man to ask, "Why?"

Gathering a single drop of energy, Andrei spoke his last words, "This life is not worth living." Then, he slipped away, unconscious.

Aware of the importance of such an unexpected event in that small neighbourhood, the superintendent returned to the crowd. Hiding his own emotions, he said loudly, in a cold, careless voice, "Andrei tried to kill himself! Another fool is dying because of drugs. Someone call an ambulance…"

No one did, so trying not to lose control, with his cell phone awkwardly in his hand, he dialed the number while heading back to his office. All heads turned towards him, all eyes staring at him while he walked. He felt overwhelmed by a heavy caring.

Making her way through the crowd, Andrei's childhood friend, Alexandra, heard the superintendent's words. She wanted to say something but did not have enough courage. She looked in silence at her poor friend. She felt bottled up and struggled for the words that might express her feelings: *"Go to him! Stay beside him! Let him feel your love! Don't leave him alone in front of death!"* But how could she? She was so afraid! Andrei was no longer the friend filled with the joy of life who shared his dreams and hopes with her. She would remember him as a happy child and a free spirit though. She would not allow this image of him to take away what he meant to her.

She muttered over and over, *"Please, God, be merciful! Save him! We need a miracle!"* But deep down inside her, she knew that it was impossible for Andrei to survive. He lived on the 9th floor, had fallen that far, and she could not understand what unknown force was keeping him alive, prolonging his suffering. Yet she tried not to accept this morbid reality, desperately ignoring her rationality, desperately ignoring the cruel truth. She grasped for something to hold on to and, for the first time in her life, she found herself in a mystical situation, wishing for a pact, a bargain…anything with God. The sound of the ambulance was the only answer she got. Powerless, she left the scene while the paramedics carried Andrei's body to their vehicle.

Avoiding her neighbours, Alexandra went to the other side of the building, to the playground. She wanted to be alone, to lean on something. She threw her body on the first swing she reached. Along with wild tears on her cheeks, memories of the first time she met Andrei started to play in her head.

Through her recollection of spring times past, she saw herself as a young girl, waiting for the swallows to come back. Even now as an adult, she could not find the explanation for how, in a world built with cement and glass, a pair of swallows could build their nest on the balcony of a building.

Alexandra was jealous that these elegant, beautiful birds had not chosen her balcony for their home. Instead, the family, a husband and a wife, who lived beside her, had this privilege. At least for a few years she was happy because none of them disturbed and harmed the flying couple. That spring, her neighbours had moved out and Alexandra had become worried, thinking of the swallows' fate.

From time to time she checked the next balcony to see if the swallows returned or to find if the new tenants were finally there.

One day, she was surprised at the sight of a boy who looked

curiously at her from beneath his eyelashes. Alexandra started a conversation with this new neighbour, advised him about the swallows. Impatient in wanting to be liked by her, the little boy promised that he would take care of the swallows.

Then he introduced himself as Andrei.

Raised by his older sister and his hard working mother, Andrei had come to the neighbourhood when he was eight years old. He was a shy boy with shining black eyes and a beautiful smile. He enjoyed living within that tight knit community, mothers and children spending time together, helping and taking care of each other. He stood out, his manners and kindness embraced by all.

In a short time, he made a lot of friends, but his favorite was Alexandra, even if she was a girl and four years older than he. Gradually, he became a genuine part of her life.

In the beginning, he followed Alexandra like a puppy, like her faithful shadow. Every morning Alexandra woke up to Andrei calling her through the thin glass wall that separated their balconies. Laughing, they prepared for school. Always, they were late because they stopped on their way, either to play or to look at something interesting: an unusual shape of a tiny rock, a tree to climb, a flock of pigeons, snails patiently carrying their homes across the road.

Alexandra's parents and Andrei's mother were amused by their friendship and encouraged it. Alexandra did not have siblings and this unexpected playmate banished a special kind of loneliness from her life.

On the other hand, Andrei's mother was glad that her little son could be looked after by Alexandra's parents, because she came home late from her job.

Starting to discover the world of books, Alexandra took Andrei on imaginary adventures. One week, they were pirates, the next they turned into heroes from Greek mythology, and for almost a summer they decided to be explorers. The parks became tropical forests, islands, mountains and prairies.

One day, too tired to run or to figure out new games, lying on a bed of grass, the two friends were chatting and dreaming with open eyes. Letting Alexandra's long hair pour through his delicate fingers, Andrei spoke about his lost father. He never cried in front of her and she was wondering how a child could easily accept the losing of a parent. In a way, she misjudged him until he disclosed how much he wanted to be like his father. To become a biologist, to play guitar, to prepare delicious crêpes, to have a beautiful wife and two kids, a boy and a girl—these were Andrei's naïve goals for the future, following his paternal example. On cue, Alexandra replied that she did not want to get married because she would be a famous actress or a teacher and most importantly she would travel the world. They laughed a lot, imagining how funny Andrei would look as a serious biologist, or Alexandra carrying luggage and wearing her high heels everywhere she went.

Finally, high school opened its arms to Alexandra. She became busy with her new life and spent more time with her girlfriend. Even so, she helped Andrei with homework when he needed it. Sometimes, she was amazed to find in her coat pocket some special gift put there by him. Her old box with souvenirs still had a small jade turtle, an oyster shell, a white pressed magnolia, a swallow's feather and a little angel doll.

Alexandra recalled that times were different during their childhood; the world felt more stable. Like most children, they did not have worries or responsibilities. They were surrounded with love and protection.

But a single event occurred which would come to shadow their happiness. One day, the swallows did not return anymore. Perhaps the pollution or the increasing noise in the neighbourhood drove them away. A nature lover, Andrei suffered at the thought that other living creatures—butterflies, snails, frogs and grasshoppers—did not have a chance to survive in that harsh environment. To cheer him up, in secret, Alexandra planned to use all her savings to buy him a guitar.

Finally, on Andrei's fourteenth birthday, Alexandra unveiled her present to him. She made a joke, told him that the guitar would brighten his days when she wouldn't be nearby, for she was leaving town in a week. Puzzled, Andrei found out that she would be going to the capital city to study at a famous university.

Without Alexandra around, Andrei immersed himself in playing the guitar while he was completing high school. During the holidays he went on trips to the mountainous region of the country to be more in touch with nature and to better observe it. He was not an 'A' student, despite spending a lot of time in the library.

It seemed that he was almost about to fulfill his dreams; however, life had a different destiny for Andrei. Soon after his sister got married, their mother got sick. He was forced to give up his studies. His uncle offered him a job in typography to earn enough money to support his ill mother and himself. He agreed, considering that it was a small compromise until he could find a better solution to survive and continue his studies.

After some time, his mother's illness escalated and it became imperative to pay the debts on time. No matter how hard he tried, Andrei continued to struggle. He could not find a moment to breathe, and step away from his problems. His youth was passing him by in poverty and desperation.

Andrei was never ready to accept the journey through adulthood, never ready for harsh reality. He could not find the strength to build a bridge between his needs and what was offered to him by the world. At that point, drugs entered his life. Exotic places without worries where everything was easily achieved rescued him anytime he was stuck in depressive feelings. Finally, he had a shelter. But madness came over him every time he went there, exhausted by the race to borrow and steal, the crazy rhythm to his life.

The neighbourhood soon became fed up at the sight of his bloodshot eyes and with his turbulent attitude. Many times, through the walls, shouts were heard coming from Andrei's apartment, disturbing the sleep of his neighbours. When he met them in the elevator, Andrei became aggressive, called them names if somebody dared to ask him why he was behaving like this.

Complaints flowed into the superintendent's office. At the insistence of Andrei's sister, the superintendent promised not to call the police right away, giving some time for the young woman to solve her mother's and drugged brother's situation. Unfortunately, none of them had any idea that for Andrei it was too late.

Unexpectedly, some years later, Alexandra came back to visit her parents. She was married and expecting a baby. She was shocked to find the people gossiping about Andrei. He ignored her every time she tried to get in touch with him. Her friend was now a stranger.

But one day Andrei woke up late. A feeling of emptiness was eating him up like restless worms hang on a corpse. There was no way to escape. There was no way to hope. There was no way to smile. There was no way to cry. Overtaken by a suffocating weakness, he hurried to the balcony. The spring fresh air slapped his face. It was too much. His choice was made before he even knew it.

It took him only a few seconds to fall from the balcony and hit the ground.

THE BLOOD STONE
Chris Cameirao

The realm of Velatos was going through tough times; evil acts had spread like wildfire. Caravans had been raided by bandits seeking to sate their never-ending greed. Demonic creatures continued their uprisings against mortal men.And various kingdoms had begun to war with steel and sorcery for dominance of the land. The Kingdom of Harven was no exception to this madness. The land itself was far away from the mainland, so attackers could never reach it, but demon raids were a threat to the kingdom's security. These creatures had attacked countless villages, raided passing caravans for their goods and money, and fed on the blood spilled by their own hands. Emperor Harven couldn't stand the thought of his people being slaughtered. Nor could he stand the fact that his army was incapable of holding off the attacks.

He called forth his advisors and generals to discuss a plan of action. It was on that day a group of demon hunters was formed. The members of this group consisted of the land's finest warriors, hunters and arch-magi.

The newly-formed Slayers of Harven headed out into the land, destroying or subjugating any demonic opposition that challenged the peace. Demon attacks then began to dwindle and order to return the kingdom. The demon hunters set up their camp at the base of Mount Zenebar, in the southern part of Harven, to watch over the kingdom and its surrounding land. Mount Zenebar was a beautiful place. Forest covered the base of the mountain, flowers bloomed through the plains to the north, and Zenebar Falls poured out pure, clean water. On this land, they constructed their village. The humans, elves and dwarves of the village focused on their powers of steel and magic to subjugate and destroy demons, as well as performing acts of science to promote the kindgom's living. Such sciences included making weapons and armour from demon bones or scales, medicines from demon blood, and demonology.

At Zenebar Falls, the children of the village would play amongst the trees or swim in the lake. The children had been restricted to this area and the village. They couldn't go beyond for fear they would end up as prey to wild animals or hungry demons. Amongst the children was little Yume.

He was only ten years old. A half-Elven child with blonde hair and green eyes. He also had the Elven trademark, pointed ears that stretched back from his face. Yume had a special tree at the falls. He could tell it from the others because there was a tree house high up in the branches. There was a rope ladder there for anyone to climb up and an Elven sigil carved into the tree.

Yume sat on a rock in front of the tree. He placed his hand on the sigil and rested his head next to the tree. Yume was now able to spiritually speak to the voices of the forest. They spoke to him about what was happening in the forest.

* * *

Inside the tree house, Yume's twenty-year-old sister, Kurisu, was sleeping. She was wearing a long-sleeved tunic her mother had given her. The top half of the tunic was purple, with snowflake designs. The bottom half had an ocean wave design. Underneath the tunic was a full body suit that the demon hunters wore in battle.

Kurisu was dreaming about a night six years in the past. On that night, her family was traveling in a caravan to the village with supplies from the Emperor's castle. The whole family traveled in the old wagon, with Kurisu's mother and father in the front controlling the horses. In the back, Kurisu and her brothers watched over the goods to make sure nothing fell off or broke.

She could remember her parents' like the back of her hand. Their father was a human with black hair, brown eyes, a strong muscular build and a short beard. He carried on his back a large two-handed sword with a blade made from unmeltable ice. Their mother was a beautiful Elven woman with blonde hair and green eyes. Their father was trained to combat any demons that attacked at night. Their mother was a druid, a person who called on the powers of nature as a form of sorcery. The more powerful druids also had the power to change into animals if necessary. However, she was a pacifist and rarely ever fought demons herself. Yume was only four back then, so he was sleeping in the wagon. Her other brother, Hitora, was holding onto the milk jars. He was eleven.

Halfway to the village, they heard a villainous, beastly laughter coming from the woods.

Kurisu's father pulled on the ropes to stop the horses. Her mother turned around and gave a stone rune to Hitora. The stone rune contained protective magic that was used to help people hide from demonic sight. She then told him with her sweet voice, "I want you and your brother and sister to get out of the wagon and hide in the bushes. Use this rune's power when the creature comes. We will try to outrun it."

Hitora woke up Yume and they both got out of the wagon. Kurisu was stubborn and didn't want to leave her parents. "I'm not leaving. I want to help you fend off the creature!" she said to her mother as she reached into her pocket for the Blood Stone.

Her father cut her short. He turned around and looked at Kurisu and said, "We don't have time for this! Go with your brothers and watch over them. The demons at night are not something for my unarmed daughter to deal with."

"But father, what about the…"

Kurisu's father interrupted her with a brief hug.

"Please forgive me, my daughter. And remember what I have taught you!" he said as he threw her into the road. Then he whipped the horses and left, leaving his children behind.

Kurisu wanted to chase them and help them, but Hitora pinned her down. She squirmed on the ground, trying to break free from her brother's hold. "Let go of me! I want to help them!" she cried.

"Dammit!" Hitora said to her. "This isn't the time to go off and play hero. We need to do what father says!" He held the rune and concentrated on it, which caused its power to activate. They quietly walked into the forest and hid behind some bushes.

At that moment, three demon wolf men appeared from the bushes. They all had white fur, blue manes and stood on two feet like humans. They also wore black pants. The leader of the three had a scar that ran from his right eye to his chest and wore body armour.

"There is a scent of food and water coming from the wagon, Lord Vadriel," said one of the demons to the leader. "What are our orders?"

"I'll run ahead and steal the goods. You two find any children that were left off. Leave none alive! We must be fast before those idiots find out we're here." The minions nodded their heads and dispersed into the woods. Vadriel pursued the wagon.

"We nearly became demon food!" Kurisu said. "We have to go and help Mom and Dad!" So they traveled up the road back to the village.

It wasn't until they were about a quarter of the way that they heard the bell ringing in the elder's tower. They continued running until they found a group of Slayers from the village surveying a wagon wreck. The wagon was trashed, the goods were stolen, and the drivers had disappeared. The only clue left behind were giant paw prints, engraved in the dirt road. Blood stains also marked the wagon. The kids ran up to one of the Slayers and asked him what happened.

He looked down on them. "Did this caravan belong to someone you know?" he said.

All three nodded their heads.

"Yes. That large sword on the roadside belongs to our father," Hitora replied.

"I am terribly sorry. This caravan was attacked by members of the Iron Claw Tribe. A group of demon wolf men who have begun terrorize our land. It looks like your parents tried to defend themselves but to no avail. They were probably killed and taken by the beast. It also raided the caravan's supplies and stole them for itself."

Kurisu and Hitora looked down on the ground in disbelief. They didn't want to believe what had happened. Yume hugged Kurisu and they both cried.

Hitora cried out, "Impossible! I refuse to believe you!"

The killings sparked a war between the Slayers of Harven and the Iron Claw Tribe. They had once been a tribe of peaceful demons, until Lord Vadriel began to rule with an iron fist. After ascending to power, he raided wagons and attacked the villages of Harven. He even went so far as to kill his own brethren if they dared to defy him. This was the first time Kurisu and her siblings had heard about the Iron Claw Tribe and Lord Vadriel's dictatorship.

* * *

Kurisu screamed and awoke from her nightmare. Yume was sitting next to her on the wooden floor.

"You had that dream again, didn't you?" Yume said to Kurisu.

She rubbed her forehead and said, "Yeah, I can't get that terrible memory outta my head. Hell, I can't even sleep without crying, squirming around, or screaming these days. Anyway, why are you here? You should be studying for your examinations."

Yume rolled his eyes. "That's what I was doing, but Hitora's been drinking again!"

Kurisu knew about Hitora's drinking. It was the only way he could forget about that terrible night, the same night that infected her dreams. "Damn that drunkard! We all get a day off to be together and he can't get ale and rice wine out of his head. Let's go home before he does something he shouldn't. If we have time, I'll try and help you with your studies."

Yume sighed and started to climb down the ladder. Kurisu got up on her feet and looked out the window. She reached into her tunic pocket and pulled out the Blood Stone.

When Kurisu was twelve, she had wanted to become a demon hunter like her father. After she told him what she wanted to do, he gave her the Blood Stone. He also explained how it worked.

It was the ultimate form of subjugation, used as a last resort to take down a demon. For the stone to work, the blood from two beings was required. The blood could be put on the stone by any means. Once it received the blood from two hosts, it would spiritually connect itself to the two beings. After this, both of their souls would be removed from their bodies and stored in the crystal and it could not be used again. Kurisu's father also told her to only use it when she wanted to defeat an invincible foe or when she wanted to protect people precious to her.

Kurisu looked into it and spoke to herself. "Mother…father… why didn't you let me stay and use this? The conditions were met. Vadriel was apparently invincible and I would have saved you from him." She put away the Blood Stone and climbed down the ladder to the ground. After she apologized to Yume for taking so long to get out of the tree house, he held onto her hand and they headed for home.

By the time Kurisu and Yume got to the Slayer's village, the sun had begun to set. The sky was orange and the children had begun to return home. The guards who watched over the forests were changing. The stores had also begun to close down for the night. Hitora was sitting outside their house on a log. He was looking up into the sky, drinking from a bottle of rice wine. A Dwarven Slayer stood in front of him.

The Dwarves were short, stubby, human-like people. Most males had beards that reached their stomachs. Though they were small, their muscular builds and knowledge of all things scientific weren't something to underestimate.

He was yelling at Hitora. "Dammit laddie! Ye can't be a drinkin' that stuff every day, ya know? Ye should be a helpin' ya little laddie out with his exams, instead of bein' a drunk. If only the older lassie could a see ye now."

Hitora was one of the villager's animal hunters. He sold his kills to a Dwarven butcher shop for gold coins. However, he got extremely drunk after every hunt. He would do things like shoot arrows at others houses, insult people who passed by him, even sleep in the middle of the road. Many villagers had tried to rehabilitate him, but Hitora just ignored their offers.

"You look here ya bastard! It's my day off and I can drink whatever the hell I want! Now leave so I can have my pint in peace," he yelled back.

Kurisu wasn't thrilled with Hitora's manners, especially since the Dwarf had asked him politely to stop drinking. She took out one of her unmeltable ice knives and threw it at the jug Hitora was carrying. The knife sliced through the clay and shattered it. The rice wine splattered Hitora's orange tunic.

"What the hell?" he cried out, "I wasn't done with that!" He got up and went back into the house, to look for another jug.

Kurisu apologized to the Dwarf and followed Hitora into the house with Yume.

Their house was made completely of wood. Logs lay on top of each other to form the walls. Iron supports were applied every few feet to keep the them from rolling off each other. The den took up most of the space and there were four bedrooms. Each of them had a room. Their parents' room had been refurbished for their stepfather, Rooteus.

Hitora couldn't walk straight. He tripped and bumped into walls before he managed to sit down in front of the fire pit. Yume ran into his room and slid the door shut.

"Dammit, Hitora! I have told you a thousand times to stop drinking in front of the villagers! You're also setting a bad example for Yume!" Kurisu yelled as she walked up to him.

"Shut up! You aren't my mom or dad and neither is Root! Our real parents are dead. You heard me? Dead! And believe me, ale and rice wine beats mourning any day."

"At what cost? Drinking won't help you escape from the past. And, more importantly, think about your health. What would happen if you drank unpurified ale and died? I don't want to go to your grave and say, 'I told you so'."

Hitora felt that he didn't need schooling from his older sister. He got up from the floor and stood next to her.

"Pfft! Better to die with ale in hand than in the hands of that wolf demon from years ago."

Kurisu was shocked to hear that from her younger brother. In her anger, she smacked Hitora across the face, with enough force to knock him to the floor. "Idiot! How dare you disgrace our parents' name like that! Especially after drinking father's ale, you drunkard!"

Hitora got up and looked at his sister. He could see the anger on her face. He walked into his room quietly and slammed his door shut, leaving Kurisu alone.

She sat down in front of the fire pit and took off her gloves. She looked at her right hand, the one she had used to slap Hitora. It was mostly covered in bandages, except for her fingers. An Elven sigil was painted in blood onto the bandages that covered the back of her hand. "Why…why did I go and do something so stupid! Mother…please forgive me," she cried.

Kurisu's stepfather, Rooteus, walked in through the front door and closed it behind him. He had been sitting in the back of the house. He had heard everything. He was their mother's closest friend and had expanded her knowledge of sorcery. He was two hundred years of age, not very old for his race. As a promise to their mother, he had raised and watched over the siblings after their parents had died. In addition, he ran an Elven temple on the outskirts of the town. Rooteus wore a large hooded robe. He only unveiled himself to those he trusted. For, underneath the robe and hood, lay the body of a Drow Elf.

Drow Elves were considered to be the bane of the Elven society, shunned by the outside world. Most Drows had black skin, white hair, and glowing red eyes. Like Elves, they also had pointed ears. Many people in Velatos feared them because of their knowledge of the School of Bane, a form of dark sorcery involving darkness, evil spirits and the summoning of vile creatures.

He slowly walked over to Kurisu and sat next to her. "My child, I heard what you two were yelling about from outside the house. And I feel a few of our neighbours did as well. It is not easy to change a person. Nor to help him accept the truth that eludes him, no matter how bitter life for him is," he whispered. He wrapped his arm around Kurisu's shoulder.

She spoke to him quietly. "Six years have gone by since our

parents died, Father Rooteus. I want everyone to be happy again, like when Mother and Father were still living. But there have been too many problems. Yume is lonely and always needs someone around him to feel safe. Hitora is using drinking to escape from his problems. And I feel responsible for what happened six years ago because I didn't do anything to save them. I...I...am such a weak person." Kurisu burst into tears. "Look at me! I even slapped my own brother across his face! And I told him he had disgraced our parent's name! I am such a hypocrite."

Rooteus felt this wasn't a time for encouraging words. He knew that if he said anything, Kurisu would probably feel worse. "You are not weak. Let it all out! I am right here next to you," he whispered. Then he rubbed Kurisu's back and consoled her.

* * *

The stars were out and the moon was full and above the Slayer's Village. Yume was sleeping in his room. He dreamed of Vadriel and a small army of Iron Claw wolves. But these wolves were all in energy shackles, dragging themselves over to Vadriel who said to his brethren, "Soon, the power of the Drows will be mine! I can almost feel victory is in my grasp! I will go find the Drow sorcerer who carries the Book of Bane. You worthless soldiers will kill anyone or anything that gets in my way. Defy me, and I will take your heads."

Yume knew that of which Vadriel spoke. The Book of Bane had been written, over a span of one hundred and fifty years, by Rooteus. The book's element was Bane, fueled by darkness and evil. Its contents were some of the most apocalyptic spells known to Velatian kind. The book itself was considered pure evil. It had been sealed with Elven sigils to keep its power from escaping into the air. Even the most basic of the spells could kill a person easily. And the more powerful spells could destroy an entire kingdom in one day.

Anyone who mastered its power would be the most feared being in all of Velatos.

The wolves around Vadriel began to change. Their eyes glowed red and their teeth got longer. Their fur became black and their bodies more muscular. Yume woke up and screamed. "They're coming, Root! They're coming for you!"

Just at that moment, the bell on the Elder's Tower began to ring. "Everyone, arm yourselves. Vadriel is coming!" one of the Slayers yelled out to the villagers. Those who were able to fight ran outside with their weapons and armour. Some stayed inside the houses in case any wolf demons attacked their families.

Kurisu had heard what Yume had yelled. "Rooteus, stand behind me. I will prove I am not weak and defend your life with my own," she yelled. "Yume, stay in Hitora's room. And make sure he doesn't do anything stupid."

Yume opened his door and ran into Hitora's room. He slid the door shut and peeked through a small opening into the den. Kurisu then removed her tunic and revealed her battle armour.

Outside, an army of nearly sixty wolf demons rushed into the town, eager to engage the Slayers. They went with the battle plan Vadriel had discussed with them. They were to be the distraction while Vadriel escaped with the Book of Bane. Their appearance was exactly like the wolf demons in Yume's vision: black-furred and red-eyed.

Vadriel smashed through the roof of Kurisu's house and landed in front of Kurisu and Rooteus. The force of Vadriel's landing knocked both to the floor.

"Heh…heh…heh! It took me six years to command this army. I have been waiting that long for the ultimate power. Give me the Book of Bane or I will scatter your blood over the ground!" he yelled at Rooteus.

Rooteus got up from the floor and yelled back at Vadriel. "Foul demon. No one with a vile heart shall touch my tome. If you wanted to get me so badly, you should have come for me and not let others suffer. You have made this family grieve for six years because of your actions."

Vadriel snarled and laughed at him. "Pawns are weak. I only care about getting powerful and nothing more. I will sacrifice anyone or anything to get what I desire, from wagon travelers to my own people."

Kurisu had heard enough. She grabbed her father's ice sword leaning against the wall. She pulled out the Blood Stone and attached it to a socket on the tip of the blade.

"You heartless bastard," she cried. "You killed my parents six years ago. You lead your peaceful tribe to war. You have made my brothers suffer and ruined my hope for happiness. For what? Just so you can get the forbidden power for yourself. Well, too bad! I have the key to the stone box it's locked away in. If you want the book so badly, you will have to kill me, here and now!"

Vadriel laughed again. He didn't have time for stalling. He looked at the door to Hitora's room. "I don't have time to end your sorry life, woman. How about I strike you a deal!" He ran up to Hitora's door and smashed it with his claw. Yume was behind Hitora, scared and crying. Hitora was armed with the long bow he used to hunt animals.

He threatened Vadriel. "Do anything stupid and I will make a new tunic out of you."

"Are all you Slayers this stupid? A simple arrow used by mortal men won't bring me down! You are way out of your league, kid," Vadriel replied.

Kurisu rushed Vadriel and stabbed him in the back with the Blood Stone-tipped sword.

"My brothers are not gambling chips for your personal gain,

you coward," she cried as the sword pierced him, the tip almost hitting Hitora's face. He saw the Blood Stone glowing red. Vadriel grabbed Kurisu by the throat and walked to the door. After he bashed it down with his foot, he slashed Kurisu in the chest and threw her outside into the battlefield.

Vadriel walked out of the house, with the sword still lodged in his back. The Blood Stone on the tip had begun to glow bright red. "Woman, this sword of ice cannot do anything to me for I live in the mountains where this ice is found. I will ask you again: Give me the key, or perish with your comrades."

A Dwarf who had been fighting nearby rushed over and lifted Kurisu up, tried to get her back on her feet. She covered her wound with her hand and spoke to Vadriel. "Fool…look at the tip…of the blade…the Blood Stone is reacting to the blood of me and you."

Vadriel looked down and saw a red path of light connecting his heart to Kurisu's right hand. "The stone has chosen us. Your quest for power has cost you your life."

The trail of light pierced Vadriel's heart and Kurisu's hand. The stone fell out of the sword's socket and onto the ground. Then it started to glow white. Vadriel and Kurisu's lifeless bodies fell to the ground. Their souls had been successfully sealed into the stone.

Everyone who was fighting stopped. They all looked down at Kurisu and Vadriel. The Iron Claw wolves turned white again. Hitora and Yume ran out of the house and over to their sister. They kneeled down next to her. Yume cried out, "Sister, wake up! Please, wake up! I need you to wake up!" Yume shook Kurisu, but there was no reaction. No movement at all.

The Dwarven Slayer who had tried to help Kurisu patted Yume's shoulder. "I be sorry laddie! Ye sister's dead. The white stone there did somethin' and they both stopped moving."

Yume and Hitora couldn't believe what had just happened.

They wrapped their arms around each other and cried. The Dwarven Slayer looked up at the Iron Claw wolf next to him.

The wolf demon spoke. "Vadriel's reign of tyranny is finally over. We never wanted to attack this village. It was all Vadriel's idea and his quest for power. We had to follow him or be killed. But we are free once more! We will quietly leave and never bother you people again. I also apologize for what has happened to this woman." With that, all the surviving wolf demons departed the village, leaving their fallen leader behind.

Rooteus walked out of the house. He covered his head with the hood of his robe. He hugged Hitora and Yume. "I'm sorry you had to see this horrible sight, my children," he whispered.

Hitora said, "Root, why the Blood Stone? I just can't understand. The sword through the back would have killed him."

Rooteus answered, "Kurisu had planned this since your parents died by Vadriel's hands. She found it difficult each passing day to keep you two from grieving and mourning over the past. She wanted you two to be happy and she felt responsible for your parents' deaths. Some time ago, she stabbed her right hand with the Blood Stone. By doing this, she activated half its power."

Hitora looked down at Kurisu's lifeless body. "I was a fool. I thought that drinking would help me forget. But it never worked, and I didn't accept any help from others. Worse, I said something to her that I cannot take back."

Yume also looked down at Kurisu's body and cried some more. Hitora reached into his tunic pocket and pulled out a key. The key to the rice wine and ale cellar in the den of their house. He gave it to Rooteus and asked for a favour. "Root, discard this key. I have learned my lesson. I will carry on what my dear sister tried to do for us. I will also bury my sister myself. It's the least I can do for her!"

Rooteus took the key and kept it in his hand. Yume grabbed

Kurisu's feet and Hitora grabbed her shoulders.

"Alright, Yume, lift her into the house. We will stitch her up and lay her to rest."

Rooteus walked over to Vadriel's body. "I warned you Vadriel! And yet your lust for power was too great to see the truth!"

Inside the house, Hitora and Yume put Kurisu's body on her bed. They began to take off her damaged armour to wrap her wounds in bandages and medicinal herbs, necessary to keep demons and other creatures from picking up her scent and defiling her grave for food. Yume removed her right sleeve to find the bandages continued up to her elbow. There were more Elven sigils, written in Kurisu's own blood. Yume read the sigils out loud to his brother, *Hitora... Yume...my eternal love will always be your hope."*

Hitora looked at the sigils and said, "It will, sister...I promise!"

CONTAINMENT
Pedro Dias

My change of jobs seems not to have been a wise choice. Retrospectively, I could have avoided it all together. But, a man in my position does not do that.

I used to be a Field Agent, an extremely decorated Field Agent. I did things others wouldn't do, all They requested of me. But that was before I had my accident. I was not able to continue in service, in my duty to the nation. The doctors warned that continuing would bring on further injuries and possibly death. As Agents, we are to continue to the completion of the mission regardless of what obstacles there might be. But my accident prevented me from completing even the smallest of tasks and They could not afford to have that large a liability. "All for the mission" is Their motto.

I felt as though I had been ousted. Having been in service for so long, They offered me a different job, a different post. The other option was retirement with a disability pension along with the regular retirement pension. I could not imagine life as a retiree, sitting back, observing the world go by as I aged in the four-walled prison people call a home, living on a handsome stream of unearned money while the nation was in danger every moment. I immediately took the job but I doubt I should have.

My physician has instructed me to keep this journal as a way to relieve the stress of my injury. I have been told to write down my every thought and feeling so that I can later analyze what is causing my emotions. I am against the idea, because writing things down on paper leaves a trail, a trail that could be used against me if the need arises. A record of happenings better left alone.

* * *

My first day on duty and there is a strange sense of dread wafting throughout these immense halls. It is like a fog. The fluorescent lights shining down from the ceiling make these white halls brilliant, blinding, like the starched white of a laboratory. Metal doors not a foot apart make a continuous pattern as far as the eye can see, a filing cabinet of immense size for the most dangerous criminals our society has. This is what I was told, anyway. They did not tell me what crimes these criminals committed. That information is on a need-to-know basis.

It is strange that such a sense of dread should emanate from each and every metal door, as if the prisoners were having their souls tortured. These halls seem to oppress my mind. One can only imagine what kinds of emotions those prisoners must be feeling. The other 'guards' here (I do not like the term 'guard' applied to myself; it's an ugly blemish on my record) do not seem to notice anything odd. Perhaps they are numbed after being exposed to this place for so long. Although I have thoughts and feelings contrary to my stature as a simple 'guard,' I must remain uncaring or else lose my mind and job.

As an Agent, I was trained to desensitize myself, to eliminate whatever morals I had, and be the most efficient force I could be in the executing of my task. I must not forget that.

* * *

They've brought in a new guard.

This place is split up into sections, perhaps under some sort of order, and an increasingly higher level guard is placed in charge of each sector, backed by a taskforce in case any of the prisoners gets out of hand. It is rare that They change the guard of a sector because this place is high profile and is kept from the eyes of normal people. They would hardly let someone deemed unfit even set eyes on this prison.

I caught a glimpse of him during one of our 'outsides'. An 'outside' is an event where we prisoners are dragged from our cells and experimented on. He is an aged man with a hard face and as many grey hairs as he has black. Cold, hard blue eyes stare out of an iron mask. It seems fitting that a man like that should be given the task of torturing.

The darkness of this cell closes in on my mind, rips at my sanity, grips at my soul. I can sometimes hear the screams of other inmates when they have reached the edge and failed to hold on and have fallen into utter madness. I wonder when I will lose all hope and become a crazed madman screaming for my release from the hell that They have placed me in.

I thank the powers in heaven that allow the smallest amount of light to pour in from the crack in the door of my cell. It is enough to barely illuminate the tiny rectangle I am forced to inhabit.

I've been able to create a space in the flotation device in the toilet to keep this journal, my life's story. It is dry and hard to find. It is incredibly difficult to write on the small amount of thin toilet paper we are allowed, but worth it when it allows me to keep my thoughts straight, the only thing that stops Them from conquering me.

They have put us in prison, behind the bars that will hold us in place until we become mere putty in Their hands. They are the murderers, the thieves, the lunatics. They have no pity. They are the real scum of our race. We are different. They see us as dangerous. Yes, us, we who have knowledge of Their dirty little secrets. The secrets better kept from the ones They rule. They say we are the real dangers to society. And not just because of the secrets we know but because of the power we have to help people see truth. The power to make people open their minds and stop living *what they think is a life. To open their eyes to the atrocities they let pass unseen. The power They wish to have for Themselves, to use for Their own purposes.*

How unfortunate that society cannot see Them. The people let Them put a leader in front of their faces and they accept him. How unfortunate that the people do not realize it is all an act They constructed, a way to distract the public's attention while They execute Their plans. It is horrible that the people do not realize that the only power They have is the power of death. The threat to end lives. But They will not end every life for then They would have nothing to rule except worthless land and empty buildings.

But They are so desperate to keep their secrets that They would eliminate Their own. If there is a member in Their faction who learns of the truth or tires of such deception, They send in special operatives to search out and capture this person. He is taken and never seen again.

* * *

There is not much to the running of this facility. Those souls remain locked behind the metal doors most of the time. Screams tear the silence of the hall and fill my head with pity and disgust. If the screaming persists a group of men clad in black assault the cell and drag out the body of a shrivelled, weak creature in dirty, stained rags rotting from age. These prisoners seem like meek people who cannot fend for themselves.

My conscience screams in pain for them but I expertly shut it down. Still, a question floats in the back of my head, a dull throbbing ache. It asks what justice there is in this torture. The feeling of dread has now settled into my bones to the point where I feel depression and melancholia with each step I take. I cannot seem to shake off these feelings and emotions no matter my training and education.

This bodes badly for me. It is most puzzling.

The prisoners' cells were left to my searching when they were called for yard duty. In one cell, I found a flimsy sheet of toilet paper with markings all over it, writing upon closer inspection. The claustrophobic cell that the writing had come from was the cell of a prisoner who calls himself 'K2.' He has written an immense amount across a variety of subjects. Much of it has to do with things They have done. It did not make sense.

I have been told to keep my distance from any of the prisoners here but I feel the need to approach this one to find out more. What is written on this paper cannot be true. What could bring a person to draw these conclusions? I have decided to approach this prisoner about this matter, and will report him to Them if he should prove to be a problem.

* * *

I have made a grave error. I forgot one of my sheets of toilet paper. I left it lying on the floor. I had not hidden it by the time I was forced from my cell. It was good fortune that They did not come across the rest of my writings. I cannot make a mistake like that again because I will lose my life otherwise.

During our most recent 'outside', the head guard of my section approached me. That iron statue of power strode towards me in a way that signalled the end of my life. He introduced himself as "Bradard" and showed me the piece of writing in question. He went on to interrogate me, asked what my intentions were. He threatened to report me and have me taken away. I explained to him what was on the paper. I explained all the undeniable evidence of the things They have done. This was my opportunity to throw Their ranks into disarray. If They lost control of Their own members, if They dwindled to only Their topmost influential members, They could be more easily overthrown. I took my chance to convince one of Their own. He turned pale and his skin became cold and clammy as I told him the secrets. That mask of impenetrable iron faltered.

I'll be killed if he chooses to report me, but it was a risk worth taking.

* * *

The screams have penetrated my skull and skewered my brain. I search the facility for answers and solutions. I cannot get away from the soulless bodies that continuously emerge from the cells. These deprived entities crawl after me to attain what they do not have. Their hollow eyes reflect eternal torment. I have questioned my fellow 'guards' about what I have heard. I have asked if the atrocities are true, but they just stare at me with dull, lifeless eyes. They are clueless to what is happening around them. Their souls have already been sucked out; they are merely shells hastening to their own deaths, performing their duties.

I cannot allow myself to die in such a way. I would have chosen to retire first. But I must be very careful creeping around looking for answers. The walls watch me and record what it is I am doing at all times. I am sure They can see the panicked look in my eye, the yellow crust at the corners of my eyes. I search for answers to this insanity.

The accusations I have heard make sense but how can things of this magnitude be kept secret? One cannot be while the other is. I will keep on searching the vastness of this place for an answer but answers are scarce. I look through files hoping to keep the ghouls at bay. They cannot end my life; surely I am protected. I search Their computer networks for explanations. The lies staring me in the face drone and buzz in my ear like the sound of a thousand bees.

* * *

The darkness hammers away at my mind, but my writing

keeps me busy. For some time now this place has been unusually active. Taskforces have been bursting into each of our cells and doing violent searches but They have found nothing. However smart They are, They are stupid. My discovered thoughts must have been forgotten or I would be dead by now. How long can this horrid cycle persist?

They've brought in a new guard for my sector.

SUMMER HILL DREAM
Nikola Streker

I was sleepwalking through my life when she suddenly appeared before me. It was her last year in high school and she had been there all along just like me, but our paths had not crossed until then. That was typical considering the size of the school and the number of students. I never met many people even though I was sharing life with them in this old building. She was one of those people who went under my radar until she walked into the classroom. I didn't think much of it then.

It was around that time that I had a series of vivid dreams. In the first dream, I was sitting on a bed of grass and flowers. I looked up at a sky that looked like night. All the stars were visible even though it seemed that it was midday in a meadow. Then I saw a unicorn with a red and yellow mane running around freely. A shooting star appeared and it made the dream dissolve. I woke up puzzled and wondered where all this stuff came from. It was then she popped into my mind. That was the first time I thought about her.

It was not love at first sight. I'm glad that it wasn't because for me that always meant it was about physical attraction and nothing more. She was beautiful in a girlish sort of way with her pretty golden hair. I didn't speak to her until one day when I was hanging around the school with my friends. We were sitting across the street on top of a short brick wall under some trees. She walked by us and without thinking I half-jokingly asked her if she wanted to come to a party. She politely explained that she had to work that night and kept walking.

I saw her a few weeks later while I was waiting at a bus stop. I looked up from the newspaper I was reading and our eyes met. We smiled at each other. She had an angelic smile. She walked over to me and struck up a conversation.

Once we started talking, we didn't stop until the bus brought us to the school. At first, we talked about regular stuff, just getting to know each other. She told me that she lived in the Summer Hill area, very close to where I lived. She also mentioned in passing that she wanted to go to a university in a different city. Eventually, we spontaneously moved to an insight of a sort. We both noticed and commented on how the school subjects that year were connected to each other. We found it interesting that there were common themes that permeated the courses. The similarities and unity were screaming at us. Not the differences and separation. I was starting to feel that we were two of a kind.

What captured me was her effortless carrying of the conversation. I was completely surprised at her eagerness to communicate meaningfully with a guy she did not know. It felt very positive that she had taken the initiative to approach me and talk to me. I had found, from my personal experiences in high school, that girls were usually unwilling to make that first step. It was always up to the guy to think of random things to say just to keep the first exchange going. I often discussed this with girls at school and they always claimed that it was just like that naturally. My friends and I disagreed as we always saw it really being up to the person and not some dull norm. She was an exception to the rule. She was an individual. There was nothing of that awkwardness and lack of trust that initially exists between two strangers. She breezed into my consciousness like a breath of fresh air. It seemed to me like she grew out of my wishes.

Not much after this, I had another dream in which I felt the need to catch a butterfly resting on a sunflower. I observed it and rushed towards it, but it quickly flew away and no matter how hard

I tried I could not catch it. Eventually, I felt that I did not really want to capture it and chasing it through the sunflower field would be like trying to catch the blowing wind.

One day I skipped a class and ended up in the cafeteria. She was sitting at one of the tables and I sat beside her. I asked her about the Socialist Party meeting and made it clear that I regretted not being able to attend. A few days earlier she had made an announcement in class about it and I really wanted to go. She was clearly enthusiastic. She glowed while talking about revolutions. Her eyes glittered with energy and hope. I was fascinated by the light in her eyes. She was not content with the way things were and understood that drastic change was needed. Here was this girl, socially aware and politically conscious. She was the type of girl who could change the world. How could I not love her?

One thing that soon became apparent in our conversations was our mutual thirst for knowledge. She had a little, black notebook in which she wrote a lot about everything from philosophy to international politics. I had a look at it once in class and was overwhelmed by its content. She wrote down facts about U.S. foreign policy, descriptions of wars that took place all over the planet, personal comments on political ideologies, quotes by famous philosophers and political leaders. I entertained the thought that she was really a spy. Then I remembered how many times my friends said that about me when hearing one of my political rants. After reading what she had written, I made a few comments about my personal war experiences during the Yugoslavian conflicts of the 1990's. She noticed that I was informed. This made her more interested in me.

Some time later, I was walking down the hall of our school when she emerged from the crowd. She was like a mirage appearing in the desert, true colour among dark shades. She asked me to meet her at the cafeteria—just like before—to discuss in detail subjects that we had only briefly touched upon previously. She really wanted to understand the U.S. involvement in the Yugoslavian wars. I skipped the same class again because the prospect of talking to her was far more exciting than listening to lessons given by an unconfident and unqualified first year teacher.

She was eager to start and waved me over when I showed up. I unloaded my mind and she absorbed all of it. She just let my memories, opinions, and philosophies wash over her. I noticed that she began to sparkle again. It seemed as if the knowledge that she was siphoning from me into her wide-open mind was making her shine. This girl was slowly materializing out of my dreams and into reality.

One day, we were sitting outside on a bench. It was warm and sunny. The grass appeared to be like a green ocean and the sun was creating sparks on its surface. Leaves on the tree branches were golden green. Everything was illuminated. It brought out in me a feeling straight from my childhood. These two guys that I know noticed us and came over. One asked her if he could spray her with the water gun he was holding and when she declined the other asked if she would be angry if he sprayed her. They were sort-of-friends and everyone thought that they were amusing, but I was growing weary of them. They quickly moved away when she showed no interest in interacting with them. She confessed that she found them annoying. I looked at her and was absolutely captivated. The beauty of love was in her eyes while the sunlight streamed through her hair.

We were in the school library with some classmates when she started talking about the general madness of people in the world and how sometimes she just felt like killing herself. Somebody shrugged off her remark without much thought while I was left speechless. I just stared at her while she kept talking. I was stunned and amazed at her honesty. She was like a child in her openness. Nobody heard her except me. She was talking to me, to the deepest parts of me. Other people seemed deaf to her. It was then that I realized she was the kind of girl who could fit into my personal, private world.

Then I dreamed of a house. It felt like the house was me. I was sitting in a soft, red sofa when I caught a fleeting glimpse of something shiny floating through the windows and doors. It appeared big but when I focused on it I saw that it was a small, yellow bird. It chirped a song and then abruptly flew away through the window. Then two balloons flew up from behind house. The wind was blowing them in the same direction, but as they got higher the wind parted them and each one started floating its own way. The dream made me understand that she had an aura about her that rendered her surreal. She fit into an archetype of a romantic, daydream love. It wasn't a sexual urge or instinct that had guided me to her. I really felt true love for a fellow human being.

This scared me, so I decided not to stay in touch with her and she soon disappeared. But all the signs along my path were pointing towards her even after she was gone. A fellow student mentioned to me that he had never met a smarter girl. Then I saw her name written in big letters on the front cover of a textbook. That moment felt unreal. I asked the teacher about it and he told me that she had written that the previous year when she was using the book. He also had nothing but praise for her. She was always on my mind. I was being reminded of her even when I wasn't thinking about her. I could not decipher these signs. At first I thought they meant that I should contact her but I think they existed to test my decision to part from her.

TALES OF A TRAINSPOTTER
Natasha MacDonald

The stars on October 17th were masked by a murky gray sky. Light particles from outside cast an unsettling bright glow through Fleming's window that distracted him while he was reading. Every night, Fleming opened his window, just crack, in anticipation of the sound of the steam whistle engine passing through the nearby town of Plainfield. He could hear the train approach. He paused from his book for a moment to listen until the whistle faded into the distance and the squawk of the crickets returned. It was 12:34 the last time he had glanced at the digits on his bedside alarm clock, and the long hand on his stopwatch was pointing at the '22'.

When Fleming opened his eyes, still staring in the direction of his alarm clock, it took him a second to register the time: 2:22. Lying over his chest was his book, *Tales of a Trainspotter,* that his father had purchased for him on his fifteenth birthday. It was at this age that Fleming had begun to develop his obsessions. By age seventeen, he was indeed captivated by the hobby he understood as Trainspotting. As far as Fleming knew, a Trainspotter was a train enthusiast who spent his time recording each and every detail of each and every train he encountered throughout his lifetime. Some of the craziest fanatics claimed they could recall the exact details and circumstances of any particular trip whenever they saw numbers that corresponded to serial numbers of trains they had ridden. The author of his book, Leland Crocker, was one of those fanatics who believed that each trip was, at least, vaguely connected to the next and that these absolute railway connections held 'keys' to other occurrences in life.

Fleming reached for the book on his chest and placed it on the bedside table beside his alarm clock. Sitting up, he slipped his right foot then his left foot from under the right side of his bed covers and stepped onto the cold wooden floor. Placed neatly beside his left foot were his sneakers. They were still looking new, with white laces and shiny soles, just a couple of scuff marks and one dried chunk of mud stuck to the bottom of the right sole.

One foot at a time, beginning with the left, he slipped his feet into his sneakers. He bent down and tied the right lace before he shifted his weight to tie the left. On the floor, directly in front of his left foot, was his journal. Fleming stared at the page open in front of him, covered with doodles, circles and nondescript sketches and scribblings. He carried his journal and his stopwatch almost everywhere he went, obsessively recording and graphing time like it held an answer to some secret key to life. Each night he recorded in his journal the following details:

> the date and the time he had spent reading,
> the page where he left off,
> the specifics of the chapter he had read, and
> any other ideas that came to his mind.

Then he would place his watch with his journal in the top drawer of his night table before he turned out his reading lamp and went to sleep. On the floor beside his journal was his stopwatch.

Fleming picked up his watch and looked at the long hand pointing to the '33'. The short hand was pointing to the first hour mark. He inspected the watch, making the assumption he had dropped it while he was sleeping, but everything appeared to be working just fine. He stood slowly and grabbed his backpack, wedged between his bed and his night table. He stuffed his watch into the left side pocket of his pack and inserted his right arm, followed by his left, into the straps. Then he secured it on his back.

Fleming moved slowly. He stopped to open his bedroom door

and continued to the hallway. He opened the front door carefully and stood silently for a minute as he stared out onto the lawn and into the trees that cast gray shadows into the murky night sky. He stepped forward onto the porch's welcome mat. As his left foot followed, he gently grabbed the doorknob behind him. The weight of his body moving forward put the door in motion. The hinges squeaked as he turned around to catch the door closing behind him. He paused, his hand still on the knob, before he tried to turn it clockwise. The door was locked. He had left his keys inside. He turned slowly, stared into the trees, and then, without looking behind him, started down the steps and into the shadows.

Fleming ran. He ran over rocks, down rocks, through shadows, in shadows, between tiny trees and giant trees, through tall grass and short grass and over hill after hill. At one point he stopped. He reached behind him into the left pocket of his pack. He pulled out his stopwatch. The long hand was pointing at the '55'. The short hand was still at the hour mark. He secured the watch in his pack and continued on his way.

Fleming ran over the Plainfield logging bridge, crossed over Rail Road Route 7, jumped the shoal at Conductor's Stream and headed towards Conductor's Field. Plainfield was a small town located 22 kilometers, exactly 18 minutes, from Center Valley. He had lived on Rail Road Route 6 for his entire life and could recognize every inch of backcountry, even in the dark. As he approached Conductor's Field, at the southwest entrance, he noticed a dilapidated storage shed. Fleming's father had told him that farmers had built these sheds many years before to store feed for their livestock in order to prepare for the seasons that limited road accessibility for big farm equipment. The wood on the shed was aging and the roof was covered in a rust that reflected a luminous red hue into the gray lit sky. Fleming stopped running. He approached the shed slowly.

On the southwest side of the building, he noticed a door. The door was covered in mats of moss. Over the years, the moss had spread in the damp cracks of the aging wood, germinating so profusely that it nearly consumed the entire door. Between the mats of moss there was a rusted escutcheon that reflected just a glimmer of light into the night sky. Fleming pulled the moss away from the key plate to uncover the keyhole. He gently positioned his hand over the hole then, with his sweaty fingertips, chilled now from the night air, pushed and felt the door budge, just a little. When he pushed a little harder, the door swung open. Inside it was black, so black that the darkness in front of him consumed the sky that had once lit the spot where he was standing. He stood, for a minute, staring into the blackness. With his right foot he stepped over the doorframe and into the dark. He followed with his left.

* * *

The train was bright. It took him a minute to adjust his eyes. He looked over his shoulder just in time to see the doors slide shut. Perhaps, he thought, he was on a subway. The light was bleak and, although it was candescent, it cast the same murky shadows as the gray night sky. He turned to his left and began to walk down the aisle of the car. On his right he saw a young woman reading. The book she held in her hands was titled, *Thinking With Your Heart Instead of Your Head.* Her eyes gleamed with an intense concentration. She blinked slowly, as if she were resting, between pages.

The young woman had long, wavy, brown hair and wore just a little make up. Perhaps, Fleming thought, she was too young to be wearing a lot just yet. She was beautiful indeed, like a collector's edition porcelain doll, with the deepest green eyes, the palest skin, and the rosiest cheeks. She was wearing a green knit jade turtleneck sweater, a long jean skirt, and tiny white ankle socks and tiny white canvas deck shoes with little green laces that matched her sweater and the ribbon in her hair.

A hoarse voice spoke up from behind her.

'Got the time, boy?'

Fleming turned. He was looking at a man three times his age. The man wore glasses, thick ones, and a matted brown jacket with the left chest pocket missing. His hair was messy. It needed cutting and it stuck out in every direction from under his gray boater hat. His boots were dirty. They looked like the boots of a working man, and yet he sat tall and proud with a particular intelligence in his eyes, like he had had some sort of advantage that made him comfortable. An awkward looking briefcase sat beside him. Fleming stared at it for a while. He could feel the train slowing.

'Got the time boy?' the man repeated in his hoarse voice.

Fleming reached for his stopwatch in his left pocket.

'The train comes in at 3:33,' the man said.

Fleming looked at his watch. The short hand was pointing to the second hour mark and the long hand was pointing to the '11'. Fleming tried to do the math in his head. It was 2:22 when he woke up and the long hand was pointing to the '33' and the short hand was pointing to the one hour mark. He gazed down at the floor, ran the figures in his head.

'3:22,' Fleming said.

'Can't be,' said the man. 'The train arrives at 3:33. Can't trust a watch like that anyway.'

'Actually,' said the young woman from across the train, 'it will arrive much later than that.'

The man looked skeptically at her from under the brim of his hat. 'How can you be sure?'

'I just have a feeling,' said the woman.

'Can't trust a feeling...' said the man, '...or a piece of metal either. Can only trust your own head, and my head says this train comes in at 3:33! The schedule said this train runs for 2 hours and 22 minutes. We left at 1:11, so this train comes in at 3:33. We haven't been on this train for more than two hours. Those are the calculations. 3:33 is when this train arrives.'

'Well,' said the young woman, 'that is your educated opinion. But I have ridden this train many times before, and the stop at Heedsville was much longer today than any other day. We were delayed leaving the station at least five minutes longer than usual, and the stop at Feelson was at least six minutes longer than it's ever been before. So that means this train will arrive at 3:44.'

The man looked at her again, his skepticism intensifying.

'And you think so because you have a feeling?'

'I know so,' said the woman.

The train came to a complete stop.

'Intuitsville,' said the operator. Fleming watched the doors as they opened. He saw no one rise to get off.

The man continued to speak to the young woman. 'Well, I'm getting off this train at 3:33.'

As Fleming glanced through the open doors, he noticed the analog clock on the platform arrival sign. It read 2:22. He felt a jarring sensation in his stomach, and he hesitated for a moment.

'2:22,' he thought. 'That can't be right.'

Fleming noticed the young woman staring directly at his feet.

'Where are you going?' she said.

Fleming was silent for a brief second as he gazed at her porcelain features. 'I'm going home.'

'Where's home?' she said.

'Plainfield,' said Fleming.

'Sounds very lovely.'

'Yes,' said Fleming, 'it is!'

The woman nodded as she smiled gently and returned to reading her book.

* * *

Fleming sat five seats down from the young woman in the train car. He could see the man across from her rooting through his briefcase. He took his pack off his back and placed it between his legs so he could sit comfortably. He bent down to open the front zipper and reached in. He immediately relaxed when he felt a hard cover. He knew it was his *Tales of a Trainspotter* because he could feel the corner that was missing. He took the book out and opened it to the page where he had left off reading. It had doodles, circles, all over it.

Water on the Rails in 1966

Sunday 22nd July 1966 was humid. I was to travel on the 6931 North Gate Rail with 4 stopovers to Beleevton, where I was to meet my brother and my mother, then to Barlington on the Coach 76452. There were few passengers when I boarded the North Gate, at the WaterBridge Station. It was to arrive at the South entrance of the Beleevton Center at 4:44pm. There were signs that the weather might break and I was the last to settle in the rear compartment. It was the summer I had turned 18 and I was just finishing my last school semester at the Colonial University in WaterBridge.

I had made the trip several times to Beleevton before and the 6931 North Gate Engine was working well until St. Peters Marsh, where a Midway engine took over. When we checked in at the Abbison Newton terminal we were already running 3 minutes behind, but it was to be expected on a Sunday afternoon.

While we were delayed at Abbison, I had ceased trainspotting to concentrate on other attractions. I looked out the coach window, in time to notice that the skies had blackened and rain had begun to fall. After another 5 minute delay, for more checks, we were on our way. By the junction at Coveland, the lightening flashes were continuous and pulsing, one after another. The storm was raging and the water was pouring over the rails. After some time the guard went through the train, advising that the Willton Tunnel was flooded and we could have a long wait. I went back to calculating the new predicted time we would arrive in Pennyton.

I had just recorded the new speed calculations for the midway engine, inclusive of the water on the rails, when I overheard a woman asking a guard if she might exit the train. I heard the guard explain that the delay wouldn't be much longer. Then the woman explained she had no time to waste.

She was beautiful. The most beautiful woman I had ever seen, with brunette hair and sea blue eyes. She was wearing a business suit, rare for women at the time. So I knew she must have had qualities that most other women at the time did not.

I heard the woman tell the guard that she had taken the trip several times before. She knew that with the water on the rails it would be faster to hail a driver to take her the rest of the 5 kilometers to Beleevton. The guard unsecured her luggage from the overhead rack and handed one green handbag to her. He wished her good luck as she exited the train.

At 4:46 the midway engine dropped into first gear

*and after a shove we were on our way the rest of the 5
kilometers to Beleevton. By my calculations we would
be arriving exactly 11 minutes late at 4:55, at the South
entrance of the Pennyton Center. I never saw that woman
again.*

As the train came to a stop, Fleming glanced up from his
book.

'Yep, 3:33,' the man said, as he looked out the doors onto
the platform. 'Yep, 3:33,' the man repeated as he put his right foot
forward, then his left. The doors closed behind him and he was
gone.

Fleming looked at the young woman who was still reading.
He returned to his book until he felt the train slowing again. When
he looked up he saw the woman pack her book neatly into a green
purse. She rose and gripped the riding handle to gain her balance.
Fleming quickly packed his book into his pack and slipped it on to
his back. He rose to exit the door exactly ½ a car length away from
the woman. When the train came to a complete stop, the doors
opened. Fleming stared into the shadows as he stepped over the
gap, his left foot followed by the right.

* * *

The train was bright. It took him a minute to adjust his eyes.
He looked behind him just in time to see the doors slide shut. How
peculiar, he thought, was he on another train? The light was gray
and bleak and it cast the same familiar shadows. He turned to his
left and began to walk down the shaft of the car. On his right, he saw
the young woman with the green purse. She held the same book
in her hands, *Thinking With Your Heart Instead of Your Head*. She
had the same green eyes, wore the same green laces and the same
green ribbon in her hair. He turned to see the man with the same

thick reading glasses and the same awkward briefcase, sitting across from her. Fleming stood silently, looking puzzled.

'Got the time boy?' the man said with the same hoarse voice.

Fleming continued to stand, puzzled.

'Got the time boy?' the man repeated.

'Yes,' said Fleming. He reached for his stopwatch.

'3:22,' Fleming answered, as he stared at his watch.

'Can't be,' said the man. 'The train arrives at 3:33. Can't trust a watch like that anyway.'

'Actually,' said the young woman from across the train. 'It will arrive much later than that!'

Fleming stood silently, deep in thought. Their voices faded into the shadows. Between his thoughts he could pick up pieces of their conversation like interference over a radio.

'I just have a feeling...' said the young woman.

Fleming stood still.

...'that is your educated opinion. But I have ridden this train many times before, and the stop at Heedsville was much longer today than any other day...'

Fleming felt the train slowing.

'...I know so,' said the young woman.

'Intuitsville,' said the operator, as the train came to a complete stop.

'Well, I'm getting off this train at 3:33,' the man said.

Fleming stared through the open doors at the analog clock on the platform arrival sign.

'2:22,' Fleming thought to himself.

'Where are you going?' The young woman was looking directly at Fleming.

'I'm going home.'

'Where's home?' she said.

'Plainfield.'

'Sounds very lovely.'

Fleming hesitated before he smiled at the young woman. She returned to reading her book. Fleming situated himself in a different seat this time, exactly seven seats away from the man and his briefcase. He placed his pack on the floor and bent down to unzip the front pocket. As he reached into his bag and felt the hard cover of the book with the missing corner, he noticed a dried chunk of mud on the floor beside him. He took the book out and opened it to the page where he had left off.

71 Seconds in a Minute

On the 23rd of November 1966, I traveled on the 46372 southbound Royal Rail from the City of Brighton to Headsville Midland to Marksville. I had intended to record the performance of the locomotive and calculate its speed by recording the milepost timings.

I had traveled from Birston Valley to Winters Corner on the 8970 Queen Terra VI, to Midland, on the Villa 3-8 2T, # 66738, arriving at 10:13am, giving me a connection to the Royal Rail, booked to depart at 10:24. But during that 13 minute period, I had succeeded in dropping my stopwatch. A quick check revealed that everything seemed to be in working order.

8970 Briston Valley turned up a few minutes late with the usual 18 coach load, and we were away at 10:31, with 7 minutes to make up. With a relatively poor running speed at 63 mph, we didn't seem to be doing very well. My stopwatch recorded that we had taken 74 minutes 23 seconds to reach Marksville, including the time lost by a p.w. slack at Headsville.

Exiting the platform, I glanced at the clock on the Marksville arrival sign and noticed that it had stopped. Or so I thought. It was showing 12:34 when according to my stopwatch it was 12:45. If 12:34 was correct then we had traveled to Marksville in 63 minutes instead of 74. It occurred to me what had happened. I had damaged my stopwatch and, although it was working properly, it was running at the wrong speed...

Fleming felt the train slowing down. He saw the man rise from his seat and turn toward the exit doors. Fleming stuffed his book into his pack, stood as he slipped it over his shoulders, and headed towards the exit doors directly in front of him.

'Yep, 3:33,' the man said.

The doors had opened. Fleming put his right foot over the gap.

'Yep, 3:33,' he heard the man repeat as he put his left foot into the murky shadows.

* * *

The train was bright. Fleming took a minute to adjust his eyes. He looked behind him in time to see the doors slide shut. As he rubbed his eyes, the same murky shadows began to clear. He immediately turned to the left. On his right he saw the young woman, holding her book. Across from her was the man with the briefcase.

'Again?' Fleming sighed.

'Got the time, boy?'

Fleming did nothing.

'Got the time boy?'

'Yes,' said Fleming. 'It's 3:11.'

'Sounds about right,' said the man. 'The train arrives at 3:33...

although you should never trust a watch like that anyway.'

'Actually,' spoke the woman. 'It will arrive much later than that...'

Fleming stood silently. He felt his thoughts retreat deep into his stomach.

...'that is your educated opinion. But I have ridden this train many times before...'

Fleming felt the train slowing down.

...'I know so,' said the woman.

'Intuitsville,' said the operator as the train came to a complete stop.

'Well, I'm getting off this train at 3:33,' the man said.

Fleming looked through the exit doors towards the clock on the platform arrival sign. He did not hesitate as he secured his pack on his back and ran, managing to slip through the doors just before they closed.

* * *

The fog was thick. Fleming took a minute to adjust his eyes. As it cleared, he could see that he was no longer on the train. He was standing on familiar wood staring into the murky shadows cast by the trees in front of his porch. Fleming turned towards the door. The key was still inside. He sighed as he reached for the knob. He was silent for a moment before he turned the knob, clockwise. The weight of his body moving forward put the door in motion. The hinges squeaked. He paused, his hand still on the knob. He turned slowly to look out—one last time—into the gray sky and, without turning around, he put his right foot then his left foot forward, over the threshold and away from the shadows.

He pulled the door closed behind him. But it stayed open, just a crack.

THE TOWER
Zak Kain

It is the night of November the Thirteenth in the Year of our Lord 1187. I am writing this manuscript after the events that occurred this past eve at Hochdorf Tower, an attempt to set down for all what happened there. So, before you discard these words as the idle musings of an unentertained mind or ravings induced by an over-indulgence in drink, heed them, and read to the finish. It is far better to ride with caution than to blunder forth into the night unprepared.

It is my most fervent hope, though, that these notes need never be read.

* * *

There were just the two of us, in the beginning. Me, Garlain of Esterbrook, a Knight of the Temple of Solomon, and my companion, Balian of Ibelin. Balian was a Syrian Christian, and a noble in the court of the Holy Land. After the defeat of King Guy by Saladin, my companion was exiled, and so it was that he came with me back to my home, the foggy Isle of Wight.

On our way back to my ancestral holdings on that enshrouded Isle, we took a circuitous route through the wildlands of Germania, coursing through forests and fording great rivers. We drank in the exotic sights; our progress was slow. One evening, nearly two fortnights ago, we encountered a wayward troupe of traveling minstrels who happened to be taking the same route north as our party. They traveled with us along our path, and we were grateful for their company.

We rode in our wagons by day and, by night, we camped under the canopy of the forest, telling tales to one another. Then, on the fifth night, I heard the tale of Hochdorf Tower. I shall relate the tale in full, for it is important to my current plight.

THE TALE OF HOCHDORF TOWER
(As told by the wandering minstrel Midon)

In the age after the fall of the Pax Romana, near the time of Odoacer's sacking of Rome, there lived a Celtic chief whose name is now forgotten. In his lifetime he waged war on many other tribes, and large tracts of land fell under his control through his cunning and his guile. After a long life of warmongering, he had subdued all of the surrounding tribes under his rule. His warriors were vicious, and they earned his tribe the name of Skoll-kin, after a mighty wolf of legend.

One winter, during a long campaign, he and his guard entered the Eastern reaches of this forest. It is said that here he met a withered old crone who went by the name of Hildir. She dwelled in a cave under the earth and was reputed to be older than the stones themselves.

The story goes that the king dishonoured Hildir within her abode, and she cursed him to be forever weary and never to rest until he had repented his sins, in war and in hospitality.

Of course, the king ignored the warning, and continued his campaigning. He was already quite an old man by this time, so the degeneration of his mind and his body was overlooked by most. He grew weaker and, as the years passed, he retained less and less control over his kingdom, his tribe, even over his own faculties. But while he grew weaker, he lived on, spending many years in anguish.

When the king died, he was interred in a great stone

tower, called Hochdorf, purportedly not far from the fell witch's hole. It is said that he was buried with the riches of his kingdom, chalices and treasures more valuable than any other on this earth. This custom was not common at the time, and many were wary of the consequences of such a burial, for the Celtic way was to bury their lords in great mounds beneath the earth, so as to better commune with their governing spirits.

Shortly after the king's death, the frail coalition of Celtic tribes disintegrated and its members returned to a state of petty squabbling and internecine warfare.

And no more was ever told of the nameless king or his misfortune. Some say that he did not die, but wanders still the borders of his domain, never straying far from Hochdorf Tower, unable to rest, cursed to live out a shadowy half-life. Others say that he was consumed by his self-pity, his anger, and was not buried, but simply disappeared into the night when his time arrived. Still others believe that there was no witch Hildir, no mythical castle of Hochdorf, no curse, and that the king was a benevolent and kind lord who fell prey to scheming courtiers and treacherous kin.

It seemed to me after the telling of this story that something was left unsaid, but I did not press, for it had been nearly dawn, and we were anxious to leave the oppressive damp of the forest.

We made good time the following fortnight of our journey, skirting the heel of the Bavarian Alps and reaching the edges of the Black Forest. The trees were close, and our pace slowed nearly to a crawl. Then winter fell upon our sad caravan without warning. Cold winds rattled through our tents and wagons and the first snow fell early on the tenth of November. It was then that the paths of Midon and his minstrels and my companion and I diverged. Balian and I bid them farewell, and they drove on north through the blinding snow. We trudged on along the road, keeping our eyes open for shelter for the night.

After many hours traveling through snow and wind, we came upon a sombre village, called by its inhabitants Hogsdur. There we re-provisioned and rested, and planned to wait out the storm. When morning came, however, we saw to our dismay that the village had been entirely inundated; the snow was several cubits high in places. The townsfolk murmered of curses and demons, but I scoffed to my friend and made fun to lift our spirits.

However, he looked at me with fearful eyes and sat me down on a log to speak. He warned me: "Do not mock that which you do not understand, friend. There is something unnatural about this weather. This storm is wholly uncanny. I can feel it."

I replied, "I never took you for a superstitious man, Balian. There is not often snow this early in the year, but it does happen. Think nothing of it."

"Look at the villagers, companion," he continued. "They are on edge, wary. They make signs against djinn who might possess them. Do not dismiss these folktales, for they usually contain some grain of truth. Have I told you the story of Alam Ibn-Wahud, a friend of my father's father? Perhaps it will open your eyes and lend you some caution."

With that stark reprimand, he began the story of Ibn-Wahud.

THE STORY OF IBN-WAHUD
(As told by Balian of Ibelin)

This is a tale of happenings in the time of my father's father, some three-score years ago. Ibn-Wahud was a head man, the spiritual guide of his tribe, the Bagar Bedouin. And so it was that one day, a man, his name matters not, came to his tent in search of guidance. The man was a fool, uneducated and uncouth. Yet, when he came to Ibn-Wahud, he dressed in finery. He held himself straight when he walked and when he sat.

And so Ibn-Wahud asked the man what was the matter, and the man replied in a silken voice. He sounded every bit the educated man. He said to Ibn-Wahud, "This man has committed trespass upon me, and I demand recompense."

It was then that Ibn-Wahud realized that this man was possessed by one of the *djinni*, Those Who Dwell In Holes. He asked the *djinn*, "What has this man done to you that you would dominate him so?"

The *djinn* replied, "He has defiled my home with his filth and insulted my house with his manner and his threats. My price for forgiveness is his soul."

Ibn-Wahud's heart quailed at this, for he realized that the *djinni's* mind was set upon this path, but nevertheless he asked, "What may I do to appease you and save this man's soul from damnation?"

The *djinni* did not respond, but instead beckoned with a slender finger and bade Ibn-Wahud to come closer. This he did and suddenly sand rose around the twain, and whirled in a mighty vortex. When it cleared, he was standing on the edge of an oasis, not far from his village, with the *djinn* beside him, in the guise of a villager.

Ibn-Wahud spun around in beweilderment, wondering where he was. He saw footprints, evidently from the fool's feet, and what seemed to be a large hole leading underground. He turned to the *djinn* and said, "If I were to bless your home, and cleanse it of what this fool has unwittingly done, will you set his soul free?"

The *djinn* replied, "If you would do this for me, I would be in your debt." He sounded displeased, but there was nothing the *djinn* could have done, for he was bound by laws that could not be broken.

So Ibn-Wahud knelt before he gaping hole in the earth, and recited prayers from the Koran and cleansed the spirit's home. As he finished, he saw the *djinn* leap from the fool's body, a whirling storm. Ibn-Wahud was rendered unconscious and, when he awoke, he and the fool lay in the dust in front of the fool's hut.

This is a true tale, and it was told to me by Ibn-Wahud himself, when I was but a boy. So I warn you, do not make light of things which you do not understand, companion, for they may well exist, and come to pass, without your acknowledgment, or your permission.

And so was the tale of Alam Ibn-Wahud, a friend of Balian's father's father, and his encounter with a *djinn*. I did not believe such an outrageous tale at the time, but in retrospect, it seemed that nothing could be impossible.

We could not stay in the beleagured town and had to press on, so we gathered our belongings and left the sombre village of Hogsdur. Another day passed by without any sign of the storm abating and, by evening on that day, our hearts had grown heavy and we began searching for shelter for the night.

It was then that we found Hochdorf Tower, that bastion of evil of which I write. It beckoned to us even then, though we didn't know what it was at the time, a dark form rising to the heavens against the blinding snows that whipped across our faces. We ran for it across a sturdy stone bridge, out of the forest and onto a small isle, where the Tower itself stood. We found the door rotted and broken in so we quickly ran inside and found a space suitable for a fire.

The interior of the tower was inviting. Rich tapestries adorned the walls of the first level. The hearth was solid and there was an ample store of wood beside it, albeit mostly old and rotted away. But somehow even the stone walls did not break the fierce chill and, every now and then, sharp gusts of biting wind whistled up the tower...through the broken door, up the stairs at the far end, and to and fro across the stained-glass windows on the upper level.

Night fell, and Balian and I huddled close to the fire, but soon the wood ran out. Neither of us was willing to go outside in the storm in search of more, so we resigned ourselves to a cold night's sleep.

I awoke in the middle of the night with a cold sweat upon my brow. Balian was not in the room, but there was light coming from the stairwell to the upper chambers, which we had not yet explored. I took up a torch and crept up the stairs. There I found something I cannot, even now, fully believe.

Where the first level was bare and cold, the upper hall was lavish, and a warm wave of heat swamped me as I crossed the threshhold. As with the lower, tapestries covered every wall, and there were rich rugs of bearskin and braziers with torches scattered all about the floor. But what shocked me was the *gold*. Piles of it, clusters in every corner of the massive room. Bullion, coins, chalices, vases, rings—all strewn about the hall. And in one corner, Balian, running his hands through the flowing metal pieces with an expression of awe pasted upon his face.

I ran up to him and put my hand on his shoulder. He spun around and rose to his feet, and I could see in his eyes that something was not right. He looked wild, like a crazed man who had gone many days without food or drink. He stumbled back from me, tripped, sprawled on the ground, and crawled away on his back, intense fear plain on his face.

I smiled at him and said, "Why do you shrink from me, friend? What is the matter? We should be joyous!"

He replied in a hoarse whisper that was barely his own. "Back! Away from me, demon! I see you! Back!" His eyes flicked back and forth between me and a small doorway at the end of the room. I stood still a moment, fighting two urges: to wallow in the wealth that was lying before me, to claim it as my own, or to discover what was behind that dark door.

I shook my head clear and strode towards the door, down the long hallway. The light grew dimmer; there were fewer torches on the walls. By the time I reached the threshhold, only my own torch, and the glitter of coins below my feet, remained to light my way. I pushed on the door with my hand and it swung open easily. It did not creak. The room beyond was pitch black and, perhaps by chance, perhaps not, my torch sputtered out as I stepped beneath the stone arch, into the darkness.

There were no riches in this room as far as I could tell. I stepped forward, cautiously, and felt bones crack under my boots. My hands stretched outward to feel for obstructions. In this fashion, I made my way to the back wall. Then I stopped.

I could not see but I felt the hairs on the back of my neck rise. There was something in the corner, something that sucked all the warmth from the room. I dared not go closer, but the strange cold drew me, just as the riches in the hall behind me had. I fumbled forward and, upon reaching that cold corner, found a locked and chained chest. A key lay on its lid. I reached for it. I knew it was *the* key because it was made of the same material as the chest—pure gold.

The key turned in the lock, liquid smooth and too quiet for anything natural. I opened the lid and fell back in horror, a dry, rasping wail escaping my throat like a scream from beyond the grave. I dashed out of the dark room and leapt down the stairs as quickly as my pounding heart would let me. In the golden room below, there was nothing left of Balian but a crumbling skull and ashes. I am ashamed that I paid him no heed in my flight but I ran out of the accursed tower into the cold night. There I knelt, at the foot of the bridge, and bowed my head.

What I saw in the chest cannot be accurately put to page, but I shall do my best to describe it. I saw a pool and, within the pool, a king on a throne of gold. The man, withered and aged, was but a skeleton on his seat. This king ruled his domain still, and his subjects were tormented and foul beings who both loathed him and worshipped him.

He held their very hearts in thrall, ruled them through their vice, dominated them through their greed. This, I understood, was what had captured Balian! He had succumbed to the lure of the foul castle, and it was he that I saw in the depths of that pool. My friend Balian, bound with chains, bound to the king's throne, doomed to an eternity without rest, and without sleep.

It was at this moment that I realized where I knelt—Hochdorf Tower, home to an undying king, cursed, along with his treasure, by an agent of Satan.

I, who had scoffed at the minstrel Midon's tale, I who had dismissed Balian's tale of *djinn* and curses, was the one who survived that place. *It should have been me!*

I wept for Balian and I wept for the people of Hogsdur who had undoubtedly been enslaved, lured to that town over the years, one by one, and sentenced to a grisly undeath, spirits trapped within that crystal sphere. For them I wept.

* * *

This is a full chronicle of the happenings of my last fateful weeks. Nothing is omitted so, should I fail in my task, this record *must* survive, that others can be prepared. It is clear to me now, clear what must be done. I shall go back to Hogsdur, find a priest, and return to this tower in attempt to cleanse the evil within Hochdorf. If I am successful then I shall destroy this message, so that word of this abomination is never spread.

If you are reading this now, then I have failed in my task, but all hope is not lost. The deed now falls on your shoulders, reader of this chronicle. May God have mercy on your soul.

I go.

CONTRIBUTORS

Chris Cameirao was born on July 1st, 1986, at Women's College Hospital in Toronto, Ontario. When he was nine months old his family moved to Markham, Ontario. He has one sibling, an older sister, Michelle, who works in Public Relations. Chris is a student in the Computer Programming & Analysis program at Seneca@York. He hopes to get a job in Software Development. The idea for "The Blood Stone" came from his fascination with fantasy stories and games. The difficulty in writing the story was making it relate to the real world. He hopes that, one day, he will be able to make something more of it.

Claudia Cion was born in Bucharest, Romania. Pregnant with her second child, she came to Canada six years ago to start a new life. Today, she has two daughters. At her first opportunity, she enrolled as a Digital Media Arts student at Seneca@York. "In my third semester," she said, "I had the opportunity to take the Creative Writing Seminar where I fulfilled one of my dreams…writing. However, writing in English was a big challenge. But thanks to my professor, Brian Flack, my tutor, Brad Nicolau, and my colleague, Charlene Moes, I managed to write a couple of short stories. Both were based on real facts. Imagination filled out the script."

Dan Cox was born in Guelph, Ontario, in 1985, the youngest of two boys. In 1990 his family moved to Hamilton, Ontario, where he grew up. When he finished high school, he enrolled at Mohawk College to study Graphic Design and to learn more about art, his primary inspiration. Afterwards, he came to Seneca@York, to study traditional animation. "During my second semester," he notes, "I attended the Creative Writing Seminar where I learned about storytelling. One aspect of this course interested me significantly: structure. I have always enjoyed pushing the boundaries of what is typically done and trying to come up with something new and inventive. So I decided to try to write a story told through two people's journal entries."

Pedro Dias is a Digital Media Arts Student at Seneca@York. "My experience in the Creative Writing Seminar was an interesting one. The workshop gave me a forum for creative release and allowed me to play with many ideas. It also gave me a way to share those ideas with other people. My story, 'Containment', is serious and mysterious in order to make readers think." In the future, Pedro hopes to take what he has learned and enter the video game industry. He aspires to design video games and eventually have his own entertainment company. But his greatest aspiration is to relax and enjoy life as best as he can.

Dylan Inksetter was born April 21, 1986. He grew up on a farm outside Hanover, Ontario, with his parents Angus and Kathleen, his younger brother Hamish, and his older sister Meredith. After completing high school, at John Diefenbaker S.S., he enrolled at Seneca@York in the Digital Media Production program. He enjoys working in 3D modeling and animation, and hopes to one day become a part of the video game industry.

Zak Kain was born in Toronto eighteen years ago but was raised in rural Ontario. He currently lives in the city and is a fourth semester student in the Digital Media Production program. He works as a freelance designer and fine artist. He is an aspiring author and plans to attend Concordia University's Bachelor of Creative Writing program. In his spare time he enjoys reading, learning 3d animation, and film.

Sean Kelly grew up in a small suburban town just outside Detroit. His family moved to Canada for a variety of reasons, and he has enjoyed his years spent in the small towns north of Toronto. In his teenage years he became very passionate where his creativity was involved. He focused his efforts on music but attempted writing in his high school years. Following that, he enrolled at Seneca@York and completed his diploma in Radio Broadcasting.

Leona Lutterodt was born in West Africa, educated in South-East Asia as well as England, and is now living in Toronto and studying Digital Media Arts at Seneca@York. "From a young age," Leona says, "I was interested in the arts and the sciences. Rather than seeking to 'resolve' this particular dichotomy, I obtained a degree in Computer Systems Engineering in the late 90s; from this, an IT career ensued. I lived and worked in the city of London, England, as a software developer, and continued with this career after moving to Canada." When she decided to attend to her creative side again, she set her sights on a career in new media and communication arts. "This gave me the opportunity to attend the Creative Writing Seminar led by Brian Flack. I thoroughly enjoyed the experience. It taught me a lot about short story forms and writing in general."

Natasha MacDonald grew up in the town of Perth, Ontario. As a child, she asked typical questions about her place in the universe and, since she could draw them, she has had a fascination with circles. After seven years of studying Communication Arts in Toronto, her questioning continues to motivate her circle theories. "Tales of a Trainspotter" was inspired by this motif and plays with ideas about "linearity and the path of our lives". Natasha was thrilled to use the opportunity to write short fiction as a "learning prototype" for her work in the future. She is currently pursuing a career in Communication Arts, fusing film, design, writing, and spirituality as vehicles for social change.

Shannon Moore was born in 1984. This event was not predicted by George Orwell. From his early life in Kitchener, Ontario, he had a passion for the arts. Creating impossibly detailed drawings of fantasy heroes and villains fueled his imagination and led him to writing stories. After high school graduation, his love of art and his thirst for adventure took him around the world, a tour that allowed him to experience the wonders of more than 20 different countries. He is currently completing his final year in the Graphic Design program at Seneca@York. He spends his summers with his parents, younger sister, and brother in Kitchener but calls Toronto home. His newest fiction covers many generations, several centuries and his entire apartment.

Conor O'Callaghan was born in the in the midst of a blizzard on December 1st, 1986, in the small town of Georgetown, Ontario. As a result, he has always loved winter—and more specifically, he has loved hockey. Music has also always been a great interest for Conor. He plays guitar and enjoys listening to a wide variety of music. Currently enrolled in Seneca@ York's Radio Broadcasting program, he has a great interest in production and is working an internship at a brand new radio station in Erin, just twenty minutes north of Georgetown. He is considering writing as a career.

Lauren Jane Penney was born in 1984, in St. John's Newfoundland and moved to Ontario at the age of 12 with her parents and younger brother. She has been drawing and painting since early childhood and, hoping to further these talents, is studying Graphic Design at Seneca@York. The story "Idle Hands" was her first writing project, set in the landscape of her childhood. It was during the work on this story that Lauren discovered a passion for fiction writing. After finishing her education, she hopes to work as a graphic designer while continuing to write. She is planning on pursuing future publication.

Ashley Rae Smith has a love for writing that began in the Ottawa Montessori schools. Fostered by this program's philosophy of building on a student's strengths, Ashley used her talents as a creative writer together with her love of the visual arts and contributed to the annual school year book. In high school she further developed her writing skills in the media studies program. Encouraged to pursue post secondary education in media, she enrolled in the Digital Media Arts program at Seneca@York. After graduating in 2006, she returned home, to Manotick, Ontario, where she continues to write short stories.

Anton Smolski was born on June 27th, 1985, in the capital of Belarus, Minsk. During the economic crush of the mid 90s, he and his family immigrated to Canada and settled in Toronto. Since childhood, Anton has been interested in the arts and history. His lineage led him to regard history as one continuous movement, not a series of movements separated into "new eras" and certainly not culminating in any "end of history" as is popularly asserted in modern democracies. Of Slavic-Litvin descent on his mother's side of the family, his father comes from a long line of Tatar nobleman who served as the elite guard for the dukes of the Polish-Lithuanian Commonwealth. During the Bolshevik revolution many members of his extended family were "disappeared" by the regime or condemned by the field triads. "Summer in the Garden" is a reflection of this history and its significance in determining people's lives today.

Nikola Streker was born on August 8, 1985, in Belgrade, the capital city of Serbia, then the capital of the former Yugoslavia. He grew up in the nearby town of Pancevo during the 1990s when Yugoslavia was tearing itself apart with military conflicts, the reason Nikola was forced to move to Toronto in January 2000. Once he received his high school diploma, he enrolled in the Seneca@York General Arts and Sciences program. The Creative Writing Seminar was one of his favourite courses since he had never attended a workshop of any kind before. "It made me write which I was too lazy to do in my own free time. The exchange of ideas during the workshopping sessions was very interesting."

Lam (Tom) Truong is a student in Seneca@York's Computer Systems Technology CO-OP program (CTYC). He was born in Toronto in September, 1986, and lives with his parents and sister. His interests include cycling, drawing pixel art, cooking and modifying computer hardware. He is also a freelance photographer, computer technician and a website designer. "While enrolled in the Creative Writing Seminar," Tom notes, "I learned a number of things: being shy at inappropriate times can be a loss; also, creative writing can be a fun and rewarding experience. But most of all I learned to respect the written word and the wonderful twists and turns of the English language."

Jackson Withrow was born in the early 80's and has resided most of his life in Newmarket, Ontario. He is currently enrolled in the Creative Advertising program at Seneca@York. With the support of his close and large family, Jackson hopes to appease his creative desires enough for him to pursue his ambitions in writing. Taking the Creative Writing Seminar during his time at Sencca@York has allowed him to generate greater technical skill and experience. The positive hands-on results helped him to enjoy writing more than ever.